The Unconditional Surrender of the submissive male

by
Ava Paulson

Copyright ©2024 Ava Paulson
All rights reserved.

All rights reserved. No part of this publication may be reproduced, distributed, or transmitted in any form or by any means, including photocopying, recording, or other electronic or mechanical methods, without the prior written permission of the author, except in the case of brief quotations embodied in critical reviews and certain other noncommercial uses permitted by copyright law. This is a work of fiction. Any resemblance to actual persons, living or dead, or actual events is purely coincidental. All characters are over the age of eighteen.

Chapter 1

Charlie wrapped his fists tightly around the steering wheel of his ex-wife's silver Lexus. It was well after curfew, and he was unlikely to go unrecognized if he were to be seen, or worse, stopped. He felt a tightening in his chest as he pulled out onto the highway and accelerated.

The night was pitch black. He was in the middle of nowhere. If anything went wrong, he'd be on his own. He kept checking his rearview mirror while feeling a tightening in his chest. He'd questioned his own motivation a hundred times or more. *Is it even worth it?* he'd wondered on many occasions. In the beginning, it had felt natural to resist the evolution of the social order that had taken place. The rapid and seemingly unstoppable ascent of the female gender in the adoption of female supremacy had completely altered the social contract. It was unavoidable, he'd figured, that some members of the male gender would resist. And he'd made himself one such voice, speaking up in support of gender equality.

There was never a moment where Charlie felt he'd become radicalized. It was, for him, a slow and gradual transformation that led to his being involved in the promotion of what was now considered the radical concept of equality. In conversations with other males, he found that he was increasingly supportive of ideas that felt dangerous, but he thought they were correct. They felt right. *Why should he be compelled to submit?* he wondered. It wasn't as though he had asked to be born male. He hadn't done anything wrong. Sure, he thought, there were endless stories and examples of the abuses committed by the male gender in the past. The so-called patriarchy. He agreed with the women who'd fought that now-abandoned social order. But why, he asked aloud in conversation with other males, should they be collectively punished? Just for having been born with a Y chromosome?

He'd read the studies, so he knew that he had natural limitations relative to the female gender. He knew of brain imaging studies that showed the part of the brain that is involved in the violent response to stimuli, called the amygdala, is larger in men than in women. And that the frontal cortex, which helps to regulate impulses coming from the amygdala, is more active in women.

But why, he wondered, should that result in his being expected to surrender his own rights? So he began speaking out, cautiously at first, promoting the idea that males be afforded the same rights that women enjoyed. It was flatly prohibited for him to do so, but he felt it was an obligation to himself and to others of the male gender. *But at what cost to himself?* he wondered.

He couldn't imagine how men had so easily given in, as he saw it, to a life of service, to an existence ruled by women. And it wasn't just the practical, day-to-day decision making that had been radically altered. It was the entire concept of what it was to be a member of the male gender. He saw younger men presenting themselves dressed in ways that he couldn't imagine for himself. In magazine ads, in videos online, and even in public he saw men dressed in panties. *In panties,* he thought, pounding the steering wheel with his fist, thinking about how foreign the concept was to him.

Recently he'd seen a young man standing in line outside a club, right out in public, and he was wearing high-heeled shoes; sheer, thigh-high stockings; and a pair of panties—see-through of course, making his chastity device clearly visible. And those chastity devices, he couldn't imagine having given in to something like that. Sure, he thought, he'd worn one initially, for his wife, Sonia, but that was in the past now.

And if the young man's attire wasn't enough, he was on a leash. A young woman was holding the leash like it was nothing, like that was totally acceptable. Charlie couldn't imagine how it had happened. He'd always been in favor of women's liberation. Now he saw himself fighting for *men's* liberation, a thing he couldn't have imagined. He thought of his K-35 anti-locking device for removal of any chastity cage without use of the key. He thought of it as a tool in the fight for freedom.

But what most galled him were the legal ramifications. The panties, well, that just came down to being a fashion choice, ultimately. He couldn't see how a man would present himself like that, but it was only a symptom. A much bigger and more important aspect of all of this was the law. He was practically white-knuckle driving on a back road in the black of night because there was a curfew. He celebrated the fact that women were now free to, as they said, *own the night,* but he wondered if they couldn't *share* the night. His having to be home early each evening in deference to the female population made him feel resentful. The nights he had been allowed out at night when he was accompanied by his wife did not figure into his thoughts in the moment.

Suddenly, the interior of Charlie's car lit up with alternating red and blue lights in his rearview mirror.

"Oh, fuck," Charlie said aloud to himself.

He gripped the steering wheel even more tightly and pulled over onto the shoulder of the highway. He took a deep breath. He swallowed hard. His heart was pounding.

Officer Daniella Fuerza, a young woman in her third year on the police force, got out of her patrol car and began to approach the driver's side of the car. In his side mirror, Charlie could see her silhouette as she approached. He noted that she had a muscular figure, tightly wrapped in her police uniform with a gear-laden belt around her hips. She employed a slow, purposeful stride that was almost a saunter. It was the confident stride of someone comfortably in command and bristling with power.

She shined her flashlight into the car.

"You're out here alone?" Officer Fuerza asked, employing a no-nonsense attitude and tone of voice.

"Yes," he replied. "Ma'am," he quickly added.

She made a dry, clicking sound with her tongue. She didn't like "ma'am," and already, she didn't like him.

"I'll need to see your identification and vehicle registration," she said brusquely.

Charlie moved cautiously, reaching into his pocket to retrieve his wallet and then into the glove compartment to retrieve the vehicle's papers. He handed her the requested documents. She examined them briefly with her flashlight.

"Stay here," she said.

He drummed his fingers on the steering wheel, watching as she returned to her police car. *Damn*, he thought. Of course, she had to be a young female cop. Most of the police were female, he realized, so mathematically it was more likely than not. But she was also extremely beautiful. He did not know why he felt that made it worse.

At length, she returned to again stand beside his driver's side window. She handed the documents back to him.

"You're out after curfew, is there a reason for that?" she asked.

"I'm sorry," he said, "it just got late. I'm just driving home at the moment."

"This vehicle is registered in your ex-wife's name?" she asked.

"Yes, ma'am," he replied.

"Is there a reason she is your ex-wife?" she asked.

"We just had, um, different expectations of our married life, I guess," he replied.

"Were you unable to respond to her command in a satisfactory manner?" she asked.

"I, uh, I guess maybe that was it, it's not really for me to say," he said in his best submissive voice.

"Step out of the car," she said.

She took a step back while he opened the car door and got out of the vehicle.

"Turn around and place your hands behind your head," she commanded.

She placed him in handcuffs, locking each of the metal cuffs tightly around each wrist.

"You're out after curfew in your ex-wife's car, not to mention she is your ex-wife. There must be a reason for that. And generally, I would say that you've been disrespectful toward me from the moment I approached the vehicle. So, we will need to take a much closer look to find out what you're hiding."

He knew better than to talk back to her at this moment. She searched him, patting him down, ultimately placing her hand directly between his legs. She paused, leaving her hand in place.

"The fact that you aren't wearing your lock right now is troubling," she said. "Why is that?"

"I don't believe in—" he began to say, and ill-advisably, he moved suddenly while responding to her.

Daniella's police training resulted in an immediate knee to Charlie's balls, up between his legs from behind.

He groaned, then collapsed against the side of the car.

"That'll teach you," she said, holding him by the back of his neck. "Don't move. Just obey. Now again, why am I not feeling a chastity lock here?" she asked, placing her other hand once again between his legs.

"I- I don't have it at the moment," he lied, trembling with a unique fear as she pressed her hand upward against his body, "I'm sorry, it's just that—"

"I don't like excuses," she interrupted. "Do you think you're above wearing a lock on your penis?"

"I, um, no," he replied, sounding unconvincing even to himself.

"OK, Charlie," she said. Walk."

She kept her hand on the back of his neck as she guided him to her patrol car and put him in the backseat.

"I'm going to want to see some obedience from you," she warned. "Start thinking about how you can show full surrender to your superiors. Otherwise, it'll it go badly for you."

She closed the car door, then went to search his vehicle.

"Dammit," he said to himself under his breath. *Your superiors,* she'd said. She meant her, and all women. His superiors, as far as she was concerned, were anyone and everyone of the female gender. The concept of equality was not going to be viewed favorably by her to say the least. He knew what she would find in his car.

After fifteen minutes or so, she returned, started up the patrol car, and began driving toward the police station.

"When I searched the vehicle you were driving," she said over her shoulder, "I found your literature on gender equality. It appears that you had the intention of distributing the information. Now, I don't think that anyone is in any danger of being swayed by that ridiculous notion. But the fact that you obviously thought it worthwhile to promote such a wrong-headed and backward ideology tells me there must be something wrong with you. But most egregious was the K-35, for surreptitiously removing a chastity lock. Is that the reason you aren't locked up? Did you remove it yourself?"

"Yes," he admitted, hoping that honesty would serve him well in the moment.

"You think a boy shouldn't have his penis locked?" she asked. "How in the world did you hit upon that remarkably stupid idea? Even for a boy, that's some ignorant shit right there."

"I, I'm sorry," he stuttered.

"I don't care that you're sorry," she said. "I'm guessing you thought it was too restrictive. But what boys like you don't seem to get is that it's supposed to be. It's supposed to be tight, restrictive, even uncomfortable, so that it is always front and center in your mind that you're meant to be subjugated and controlled. Your inability to submit to authority is embarrassing, really."

"I just think that we all deserve to be treated equally—" he began, though he knew that it was futile to argue.

"Yeah, how about you shut the fuck up for now, Charlie," she interrupted.

They were silent for the rest of the ride to the police station. Charlie looked out the window, realizing he wouldn't be seeing the outside world for a length of time. When they arrived at the station, she led him into the booking area.

"We're going to keep you here for a few days or so until we make a determination about what to do with you," she said as she unlocked his handcuffs.

One of the things that rankled Charlie most was the segregation of civil law based on gender. As a male, he could be held by law enforcement for any length of time with no more reason than the police had an interest in investigating him.

The officer ushered him into a small room and a young woman with a humorless expression confronted him.

"Hey Shayla," Daniella said, "I've got a live one for you. This boy's name is Charlie, and he is under the impression that boys should be given equal rights. Let's disabuse him of that notion, shall we?"

"It'll be a pleasure," Shayla replied. "Just leave him to me."

She turned her attention to Charlie.

"Place your clothing in the basket," she said.

Charlie grimaced, briefly thought through his options in the moment, then reluctantly began taking off his clothes.

"Everything," she said when he hesitated in removing his underwear.

"Turn and place your hands against the wall," she said once he was naked. "Stand with your legs spread wide," she said with a commanding voice.

Charlie complied while his jaw tightened in anticipation of what was coming next. She stepped up behind him and pressed two gloved and lubricated fingers against his anus. He winced at the sensation and tried to relax his body.

"You're going to learn to submit before we're done with you," she said over his shoulder as she began pushing her fingers into his asshole. "Boys who fear submission to female authority are cowards," she said as she continued pushing until the full length of her fingers were penetrating his body. "You hear me?"

"Yes, ma'am," he replied through clenched teeth.

He had raised himself up onto the balls of his feet. She slowly rotated her fingers inside his ass. He could feel her knuckles pressed hard against his body.

"We'll see," she said. "We expect some hard submission from you boys."

Then she slid her fingers out of his asshole and discarded her silicone latex gloves. She handcuffed his wrists behind his back again, and she had him turn toward her.

"We don't let you boys go around without one of these," she said as she presented an extremely small, inverted chastity lock.

He groaned at the sight of it. Law enforcement was known for employing the smallest possible locking devices. She flashed him a look of approbation in response to his verbal reaction to the device. She spent a minute or two coercing his penis and testicles into the metal base ring and forcing the negative space cock cage into place. She slid the lock shut, which made an audible click. He gasped at the sensation.

"I'm sure that you will appreciate being locked up again," she said. "It's no good for you boys to be without."

Wearing a law-enforcement-issued chastity device locked tightly around his penis and testicles was humiliating for Charlie. The base ring was very unforgiving, sized for a secure fit rather than comfort. And the inverted design entirely and completely negated the possibility of his having an erection, with the head of his penis securely locked into position by the metal device.

Wearing it made him feel like he was one of the models from *COPS* magazine, a publication that would invariably show a photo spread of a boy wearing one of the ultra-small, police-issued chastity cages. When Charlie was younger, he'd seen an issue of *COPS* that his sister had in her room. It showed a series of photos in which a male model was wearing a remarkably tiny chastity cage, a ball gag, and what looked like a circular metal cap over his asshole. Charlie would come to understand that it was a butt plug with which the model had been penetrated. Charlie also noticed that the model had leather straps around his wrists and ankles, and there was a collar around his neck. Aside from that, he had been photographed and displayed completely naked.

Charlie was taken aback by the way the model was presented. The model was clearly doing his best to appear attractive and submissive in each of the photos. There was one in particular that seemed to show the model tightening the ball gag strap at the back of his head. Charlie couldn't imagine how the model could think to make his bondage even more restrictive. He had no idea how he could be such a proactive participant in his own subjugation.

While growing up, Charlie had enough trouble with the basic level of submission required of him. He regularly felt the sting of humiliation just having to defer to his younger sister's authority. He wondered if it wasn't his sister's treatment of him that had led to his having difficulty in accepting his proper place. She had never been nice to him concerning her superior position and took every opportunity to tease and torment him about his expected obedience to female command. She was the one who had shown him the issue of the magazine, pointing out one of the photos of the model on his hands and knees, showing his penetrated ass to the camera.

"That's how boys are supposed to submit," she'd said to him. "He's wearing a butt plug, and I'm guessing that it's pretty big.

That's what is expected of you. Do you think you could take it up the ass like that?"

"I don't know," he'd replied.

"Then you have a lot to learn," she'd said.

Officer Shayla made Charlie stand against the wall while she took his photograph, which was full frontal, then she took one each for his left and right profile. He thought about the fact that the images were going to be made public on the police website, available worldwide so that any jurisdiction would have access. Any internet search of his name would now bring up a photo of him naked, handcuffed, and locked in chastity as the first result.

He was placed in a cell, and his handcuffs were removed, but he was left naked aside from the tight metal chastity device. He sat on the cot in his cell and looked up at a plaque that had been bolted to the wall. It read "Equality of rights under the law shall be denied any and all citizens whose gender identity is male, enforcing the privilege and superiority of the female gender within the United States and within each State. The discrimination of the male sex shall be upheld, and no law shall be passed that fails to make a distinction on the basis of sex or is unable to unequivocally demonstrate that it prioritizes and favors the female gender. Women shall have rights not afforded the male gender in the United States and every place subject to its jurisdiction."

Charlie realized that his life was about to be altered in a significant way. He'd thought that his views were not only harmless, but positive in their potential effect. He was about to learn the extent to which this view was not shared by the gynarchic society that had been well-established and accepted by the populace at large.

"I am so fucked," Charlie said to himself under his breath.

Chapter 2

"I did a traffic stop on this boy who is a prominent proponent of gender equality this evening," Officer Daniella Fuerza said as she reclined on the sofa in her living room. Her husband, Tom, whom she'd assigned the rank of slave-husband, had been waiting for her, naked and kneeling on the floor, when she arrived home after work. She had made certain he understood that he was never to sit on the sofa himself and had prohibited him from using any of the furniture in the house without her permission.

"That's surprising," he replied as he began removing her boots and her socks, a service he'd routinely perform upon her return home from work.

"Can you believe it?" she said. "It's this dumbass named Charlie Taylor. I was actually kind of taken aback that there were any of his kind still in existence."

Once both of her feet were bare, Tom lifted one of her feet to his lips and kissed it reverently.

"Isn't that cute?" she asked as he began kissing her toes. "Just imagine, being a boy and thinking you've any claim to equality. I don't know whether I should be embarrassed for him, or if I think it's kind of cute and pathetic. I mean, by what possible measure could a boy claim the right to equal standing? You're either obedient or you're not. Good thing you know your place," she said as she began slipping her toes between his lips and letting him suck and lick them individually. "I did have good reason to knee him hard in the balls," she said. "I love it when they try to act up. It's so rewarding to put a boy in his place."

Tom began licking the sole of her foot from her heel to her toes.

"Anyway, he'll get what he has coming to him. And more for sure in the future if he doesn't figure it out real quick. As you know, I am a believer that boys can learn if they're properly trained."

Daniella watched her slave-husband apply his tongue in worshipping her bare foot. Then she pulled her toes from his mouth and placed her other foot to his face.

"You've never thought yourself my equal, right?" she asked. "Be honest."

"Your equal? No," he replied. "I could see that you are far superior to me the moment—"

"Hold on, why does it sound like you are qualifying that as relating to me? Surely any female is your superior?" she asked.

"Well, yes," he replied. "I guess that I haven't thought about it, since I'm committed to serving you. I've never thought about equality or its absence because it's never occurred to me to think about any correlation between the genders. The female is vastly—"

"So, you've never even thought about being disobedient?" she asked, teasing his tongue with her toes.

"I've always found that it is the obvious superiority of the female that most effectively keeps me in check," he replied. "Simply being aware of my natural limitations causes me to react in a way that is compliant and submissive. I've never thought to—"

"Hmm, you're so cute," she said as she pushed her toes into his mouth.

* * *

Daniella had met Tom two years before at a party, to which Tom had arrived entirely unaware of the requirement that boys were to be naked.

"I'm sorry, what?" he'd said to the woman in the foyer of the house where the party was being held. "Requirement?"

"How do you not know?" she asked, sounding annoyed. "All males are to be without clothes. Sorry, I can't let you in unless you comply."

"Oh," he said, and he realized he was blushing. His heart began thumping in his chest. "So . . . ."

"In there," the woman said. "You'll place your clothes on any of the empty shelves. You can pick them up when you leave."

Once he'd gotten up the courage to strip naked, Tom walked out onto the large outdoor patio overlooking the pool. He'd heard of such parties, which had become popular a while back, but he'd never been to one before. Now he was trying to calm his nerves about being so exposed. He'd gotten his butt pinched three times while walking out to stand where he was positioned now.

Then he noticed a remarkably attractive woman staring at him. She locked eyes with him and held her gaze, as though she was examining him. Her expression was neutral. He lowered his focal point to the patio floor in a show of deference to her. After several moments had elapsed, he raised his eyes and saw that she was still peering intently at him. He felt his heart pounding. His body seemed to be growing warmer. He lowered his eyes to the floor again, and he could feel that she was continuing to watch him. He tried to remain calm and not show the intimidation he was feeling.

Out of his peripheral vision he sensed her movement. She stood slowly in ascending to her full height. Her head moved to give her long, dark-brown hair a toss. She paused, as though contemplating her next movement. Then she enacted a series of long, purposeful strides that ended once she was standing directly in front of him. He was struck by how beautiful she was, not only in her appearance, but in her supremely confident personality as well.

"Hi," she said in a confrontational manner.

"Hello," he replied, and felt more naked than he had up to this point in the evening.

"So why did you decide to come here tonight?" she asked.

"My, uh, *friend,*" he replied, "he neglected to tell me this was, well, what it is. I didn't know about the being naked part."

She laughed.

"So, you thought you were going to show up and remain fully clothed?" she asked. "Like, just a regular party?"

"Yeah, pretty much," he said.

She laughed again, a melodious sound he found attractive, if not slightly cruel.

"Are you nervous?" she asked.

"I'm generally not wearing, um, nothing," he explained. "So yes, I am a little nervous."

"As far as your wearing nothing, I think you should be wearing nothing all the time," she said, looking him up and down. "Your body is really nice. You've got a nice build, and all that. Turn around."

"Yes, ma'am," he said as he turned around.

She looked at his body from behind, then told him to turn toward her.

"Don't ever call me ma'am," she said. "You will address me as Master."

"Yes, Master," he replied.

He'd delivered it with a tone that suggested he was humoring her. She made a small sound with her tongue, a little clicking sound that he would come to fear.

So, what's your name?" she asked.

"Tom," he replied.

"Nice to meet you Tom," she said, though she was looking down at his body when she said it.

Daniella and Tom had been dating for almost three months when she had him move into her house.

"I require your attention more often than you can realistically provide," she explained. "I need you to be present, so that when I require your naked obedience, you will be able to provide it without any significant delay."

And it was a few months after that when she announced her intention of taking her relationship with Tom to the next level.

"If you continue to serve me in a manner that pleases me, we'll transition to a permanent, slave-husband arrangement. And so that you understand, I will have a boyfriend as well," she explained. "I think that you'll make for a perfect cuckold for me."

"Yes, Master," he replied, his mind reeling at how effortlessly Daniella had completely dominated him.

* * *

"I'm looking forward to seeing this boy, Charlie Taylor, learn to submit," Daniella said as she removed her toes from between Tom's lips. "But I'm also looking forward to the shower you're going to get ready for me now. And then I'm going to ride on your tongue for a while. How does that sound?"

"Perfect, Master," Tom replied in earnest.

After he'd readied the shower for her, he laid himself on the bed in anticipation of her wet pussy positioned above his lips, dripping endlessly into his mouth. As he waited, he felt lucky to be Daniella's property. He was certain he couldn't feel more satisfied than he did while in service to such an impressively dominant, beautiful woman. He recognized her as his Master, not because she demanded it, but because he couldn't deny that she unquestionably held such a position of power and dominance over him. He felt that his willing submission was nothing more than what she deserved.

* * *

The next morning, Tom entered the executive meeting room quietly and stood to one side of the doorway. Of utmost importance was Tom's attentiveness to the needs of his boss, Ms. Sonia Taylor. Ms. Taylor and the other four women in the room were deep into a discussion about an upcoming project, so no one paid any attention to his entrance or his presence standing to one side of the room.

He waited.

Sonia had started her financial services firm over two decades before, and she had been an extremely successful in building and steering the company. She'd named her fledging company Findom, which at the time was a tongue-in-cheek joke in reference to financial domination, but as the company grew, it became a prophecy as it attained dominance in the industry. She was widely considered one of the most powerful women in the community, with a keen eye for talent and a merciless attitude toward achieving success. Her public profile was of such prestige that she could have any number of young males at her service by literally snapping her fingers. Tom felt himself to be lucky to have been given the privilege of such a position, having landed a position as her executive assistant.

"Tom?" Sonia said at last, her piercing green eyes making him feel like a target.

"Yes, thank you, Ms. Taylor, I'm here to collect the directives on the SLK project and take orders for lunch, if applicable," he said.

"Carly, you've got the SLK updates?" Sonia asked.

"Yeah," Carly replied, and pulled a slim folder out from her bag.

"OK, give them to the boy, and let him have the—we've all had a look at the lunch menu, right? Everyone who wants something has entered it on the app?" she asked.

"We ended up writing it on a piece of paper," Merrick said, grumbling as she leafed through some papers. "The app was all fuck-ed."

"Yeah, no, I've got it," Jess said. "I didn't have a chance to look yet, so hold up a minute."

She scanned the printout, then quickly wrote a note on the form and handed it off to Tom. He took it graciously and quickly left the room. He took a deep breath once he was safely in the hallway.

"Is he the new boy?" Merrick asked.

"Yes, just a few weeks ago," Sonia replied.

"He better not fuck up the lunch order," she said.

"He's clever, I hired him myself," she replied.

"Is he property?" Carly asked.

"Property?" Sonia asked.

"Owned," Carly clarified. "You know, married or whatever. Someone's servant."

"Oh," Sonia said, "Yes. He's married. Whatever the arrangement is, but yeah."

"Well, it's for the best," Merrick said, eyeing Carly. "You don't want to shit where you eat."

"Why," Carly said, then paused, "why is it called that? No one was talking about shitting. Gross. Why not just call it *fucking where you work?* Just say, 'You don't want to fuck where you work.' That seems to make more sense."

"Is this about the lunch order?" Merrick asked in a joking-but-not-really tone of voice. "Are you just horngry?"

"What the fuck is that?" Carly asked, laughing.

"Oh, that's when you're horny because you're hungry," Merrick replied.

"Remind me not to talk to you, Merrick," Carly said dryly.

"Alright," Sonia said, "it feels like this meeting is over."

Sonia exhibited the appearance of being relaxed and effortlessly in command as she made her way back to her office. Her employees, the majority of whom were female, were loyal to her due to her being an inspiration to them. She had an air of authority that was not forced or insistent, rather she projected an attitude of being supremely dominant by ignoring anyone who failed to meet and exceed her expectations. The pressure that everyone felt in wanting to please and impress her was felt keenly by everyone in her orbit.

Tom, in particular, felt that he had to perform at his best so as to avoid disappointing her. In his mind, it was almost the level of obligation he felt toward Daniella.

"Tom, see me in my office," Sonia said as she walked past him.

"Yes, Ms. Taylor," Tom replied.

He followed her into her palatial corner office and stood before her desk.

"Your wife is a police officer, is that correct?" she asked, reclining into the chair behind her desk.

"Yes, Ms. Taylor," he replied. "Though she refers to herself as my owner."

"I see," Sonia said, lost in thought for a moment. "Owner. So anyway, my ex-husband had a run-in with the police last night. I was informed of the fact this morning. His name is Charlie, and he ended up dabbling in some foolish gender-equality business." Sonia looked pained in relating this information. "I've heard that he has been arrested. I was wondering if your wife, I mean, owner, had any information about this turn of events."

"She, well, I believe she may have been, coincidentally, the officer who arrested him," Tom replied. "She mentioned having encountered a gender-equality proponent last night."

"Interesting," Sonia replied. "You'll keep me up to date with any developments?"

"Of course," Tom replied.

"You're excused," Sonia said, and watched Tom as he exited her office.

She leaned back in her chair. The pleasure she felt in knowing that her ex-husband, Charlie, was in custody of law enforcement wasn't quite equal the resentment she still felt toward him. She looked forward to hearing about everything that happened to him while being interrogated by the police.

She'd thought perhaps he'd been too young when she took him as her husband many years earlier. He had been some fifteen years younger than herself. But she ultimately decided that it was simply his immaturity rather than his age that had been the source of the problem. Charlie had failed to adapt to the submissive status assigned his gender, and though she felt she might have been stricter with him, ultimately it was his failure to adapt, she'd decided.

For this reason, Sonia felt optimistic about the possibility of a satisfying arrangement with the boy she'd become focused on as of late. His name was Aaron, and he was less than half her age.

She'd always been attracted to young males, enjoying their energy and their vitality. Perhaps they lacked wisdom and experience, but she felt that their beautifully hard bodies more than made up for that. It was simply a matter of training them to follow her command without question, a task she thought herself capable of accomplishing. She'd hired Aaron to be her yard boy, and she'd decided to take full advantage of him over the coming weekend. She crossed her legs and gently bit her fingertip as she entertained the thought.

Chapter 3

It was Sunday, early afternoon, when Aaron came over to attend to the maintenance of Ms. Taylor's property. She enjoyed watching him work, bare-chested and wearing a pair of cutoff shorts while he mowed the lawn. She was amused by thoughts of an earlier time in her life, when young males would attempt to display their muscular development by baring their chests, like an inappropriately intimate demonstration of their physical dominance. Now, boys would have their shirts off as a show of submission in offering themselves to be observed, examined, and even objectified.

By the time he'd killed the motor of the lawnmower, Aaron was dripping with sweat and his exposed skin had a film of dust and bits of grass the mower had kicked up in its wake. He wiped his brow in what might have appeared as a pantomime of having completed a difficult job if not for the rivulets of sweat threatening to drip into his eyes.

"Excellent work, Aaron," Ms. Taylor said as she crossed the lawn to where he stood surveying his efforts.

"Thank you, Ms. Taylor," Aaron replied.

"Please," she said, "just call me Mistress Sonia."

"Yes, Mistress Sonia," he replied. *Mistress?* he wondered. It gave him a feeling of nervous excitement to call her by such an intimate title.

Over the years, Aaron had become aware of Ms. Taylor eyeing him carefully. Year after year, he got the idea that she was waiting. Patiently waiting. She'd said at one point, "You've grown quite a bit since the last time I saw you," and she practically licked her lips in anticipation as she issued the thought.

She was considerably older than him, and he felt intimidated to an extreme he'd never felt before. Women had always paid particular attention to him, but not in the way that Ms. Taylor did. She was different. Her head lowered slightly as she looked at him. *Through him* was the way he would have described it.

"I imagine you'd like to take shower after that," she said, looking at the expansive, freshly cut lawn, then back to Aaron. "You may use mine, of course."

"Oh, it's not a problem," he began to explain.

"No, it's not," she said. "You will use my shower."

"Yes, Mistress Sonia," he replied.

"Come along," she said. "Don't be scared," she added, though it caused Aaron to feel more on edge than he already felt. She made him feel like a ripe piece of produce in the grocery store that she intended to fondle before she took a large, ravenous bite.

Aaron had been inside Ms. Taylor's home only once before, and for just a brief period of time. Her home was extraordinarily lavish, and it exuded wealth and power. He felt nervous inside her home, worried that he might break something. It seemed that everything in sight was worth more than he could earn in his lifetime. Which was also factually correct.

She had him take off his shoes and follow her upstairs. He realized that it was her bedroom she'd invited him into as she directed him into the bathroom, an area that was easily twice the size of his dorm room at school.

"You'll find a towel on the rack," she said, "which is what you'll be wearing when you come out to receive further instruction."

He noticed that she did not close the door, however, and he was unsure whether he should close it or not, so he left is as it was. He took off his clothes, feeling uniquely vulnerable while naked in Ms. Taylor's home.

Aaron had demonstrated a level of obedience that had led to his having possession of the key to his chastity device, so he removed it after he'd taken off his clothes. His self-discipline was such that he was able to restrain himself from using the key to his chastity device to masturbate to thoughts of Ms. Taylor, whose immensely powerful presence might otherwise have compelled him to give in to such impulses.

He stepped into the shower, noticing that it had no door, just a glass partition that extended halfway along its length. There was a window high in the wall at one end which admitted a direct shaft of sunlight. He felt exposed while taking a shower, but he gave into the feeling as he had come to the realization that she could do with him whatever she liked. He remembered to be grateful for the privilege of serving such an extraordinarily powerful woman, knowing that there were any number of boys who would love to be in his position.

When he walked out of the bathroom, Aaron felt uniquely exposed while wearing nothing but a towel wrapped around his waist. Ms. Taylor was on her bed waiting for him, lying on her hip, propped up on an elbow with her legs draped over the edge of the bed.

"Ah, here we are," she said as she took in the sight of Aaron wrapped in a white bath towel.

He tried not to stare at the vision of her wearing a peach-colored silk robe wrapped loosely around her elegantly feminine body. Her round, generously proportioned hips were draped in the soft fabric, luring him to admire her sexually intoxicating figure. The front of the robe was arranged loosely, allowing him to see her large breasts clearly defined beneath the silky material, which was splayed open to the point that he could see the carnation-colored edge of her large, round areolas.

"I just love how the younger a boy is, the more obvious he is in looking at a woman's body," she said, smiling. "And the result, of course," she added, gesturing to the growing erection beneath his towel. "It would appear that you are unlocked," she said. "It shows that you've demonstrated the capacity to obey. How lovely."

Aaron blushed.

"So why don't you lose the towel and let me have a look at you," she said.

Aaron slowly unwrapped the towel from his waist and then let it fall to the floor. He remained standing before her with his hands to either side of his now naked body. His cock became fully erect.

"Very nice," she said. She began slowly caressing her exposed cleavage. "Your muscles are really getting some nice definition."

She observed him, slowly allowing her gaze to slowly travel down his naked body.

"Why, Aaron, you're trembling," she said. "Are you really so intimidated by me?"

"Yes," he admitted, blushing harder.

"It's so cute to see you blush like that. It's like you've never really been examined by a woman before."

"I guess I haven't," he said.

"Well, you've been to the doctor, right?" she asked. "She has you undress?"

"Yes, but it's," he said, "it's not like this."

"No? How so?" she asked.

"I don't get hard when I think about my doctor," he said softly.

She smiled at his admission.

"Hmmm," she purred. I feel that I've waited so terribly long for this. But there's no reason to be impatient now. We have all day. And more. And I want to continue studying how your body has developed."

"Yes, Mistress Sonia," Aaron replied.

"Tell me how you feel now, standing before me and offering yourself to me to examine," she said.

"It's intimidating, to tell the truth," he admitted. "It would be more comfortable for me to kneel before you."

"Why is that?" she asked.

"You're so, uh," he said, searching for the word, "impressive. Supremely dominant, I guess. You are beautiful and powerful. It makes me nervous that I will fail to be as respectfully submissive as I should be."

"Well, I think you are being quite lovely," she said. "You stand at attention so nicely, offering your gorgeous erection to me. Your naked submission is truly a beautiful thing to observe. There's something so innocent and perhaps even naïve about you, and I don't mean that in a negative way. I adore the sight of a naked boy who appears prepared to submit selflessly to my authority. It's absolutely precious. I love it. It makes me want to do the dirtiest things to you. I feel a desire to just wreck your tight little body."

She noticed his erection throb.

"Tell me about your having come to terms with your place in regard to female authority," she said. "Young boys have such a nice way of looking at it, I find."

"It's always been obvious to me," he replied. "Women are so beautiful, and I mean not just the way they look. When they are comfortable in their command of a given situation, they are just so, I don't know, amazing, I guess. It never occurred to me that I might be considered the equal of the female gender. It would be kind of embarrassing to me to pretend to think I could compete with a female. To say nothing of a woman of your stature and power and authority. Being subjugated by women feels, well, natural. It feels right. I've never really questioned it."

"I assume, since you were always rather clever for a boy that you've been a good student," she said.

"I hope so," he replied. "I try my best."

"Your best," she repeated. She smiled. "I'm sure that you do. But tell me, have you learned the most important lesson a boy must learn? Have you learned your place?"

He blushed again.

"I believe so," he replied. "I know that I don't have the abilities the female students at my school have."

"No, you don't," she agreed. "But you do have your charms, do you not? Your gender can be so entertaining to women should we decide to amuse ourselves with your talents. You know to obey an order?"

"Yes," he responded. "I do know that."

"We'll see," she said. "Come closer," she said as she sat up on the edge of the bed.

She reached out and placed her hand on his upper chest, then made her hand into a claw shape and dragged her fingernails down the front of his body. It was surprising to him how firmly she dug her nails into his skin and how abrupt she was in raking his skin, such that she left five distinct rose-colored stripes down the front of his body, from the top of his chest to just above his cock. He emitted a gasp at the sharp, painful sensation.

"Oh, you liked that, did you?" she asked. "Because there is so much more in your immediate future."

She raked her nails down the front of his body twice more before ordering him to turn around. She repeated the action down his back, from his shoulders to halfway down his butt.

"I so enjoy your reaction to me," she said. "Turn," she said as her hands directed him to stand in profile to her. She placed one hand on his hip, then the other on his butt cheeks. She made a soft, purring sound as she held him in place, then she began to spank him with her hand across his bare ass. Out of respect for him, she landed her bare hand harder than he'd have thought possible.

"Your erection is so cute," she said. "It's so hard that it remains firmly pointing upward while I spank you. I appreciate that. Now, let's have an examination of your oral skills. You want to worship my pussy, don't you, Aaron?"

"Yes, Mistress Sonia," he replied.

She guided him down between her thighs, pushing downward on his shoulder. He maneuvered in response and knelt beside the bed. She spread her legs wider and pushed downward on his shoulder, guiding Aaron's face toward her pussy.

"That's right, just like that," Sonia said as Aaron's tongue slid slowly upward and then delved between her labia.

She felt the tension that had been building for many years completely dissipate. It had been so long that she had imagined Aaron precisely as he was at that moment. She could now feel in a tangible way the tongue she'd fantasized about serving her for so long.

"Just like that, Aaron," she repeated. "Good boy."

It was over an hour, and several of Ms. Taylor's orgasms later, that she had him lying beside her on the bed.

"Perfect, really, this fantastically hard cock of yours," she said in a dreamlike voice.

She slowly stroked the length of his shaft with her fingertip, from the base to the rim of his cock head. Then she circled the rim and noticed a small drop of clear fluid dripping from the slit at the tip.

"Oh, that's such a nice admission on the part of your body, Aaron," she said. "It means that you desire my control of you to deepen and intensify. She placed her fingertips on his ball sack and pressed them gently, feeling the weight and fullness of his balls. She watched the drop of fluid slowly begin coursing down the head of his cock toward his shaft. She slid her fingertip upward, using his body's own lubrication to make her finger slick and wet and drawing little circles against the underside of the head of his penis.

"Oh my god," he gasped, overwhelmed by the sensation. His eyes met those of Ms. Taylor, now Mistress, as she'd had him call her, and saw that she was looking at him with an adoring gaze. But there was something more, something that looked like she was ready to devour him. He couldn't help noticing that her silk robe had fallen open, exposing her breasts with their erect nipples. He inadvertently licked his lips and his mouth opened hungrily.

"You want to suck on my nipples?" she asked.

"Yes, Mistress Sonia," he replied. "Very much—"

She stifled whatever he was about to say by inserting her nipple between his lips. He began to suck as she wrapped her hand around his shaft and began stroking its length.

"You may come for me now, Aaron," she said.

His back arched and his hands pressed against the bed as his hips shuddered, shaking, then thrusting as he ejaculated. Sonia watched Aaron unload in several successive thrusts, making a large, dripping puddle of thick, hot cum on his bare chest.

"Oh, my beautiful boy," she said, delighted at the way his body now trembled, looking spent and exhausted.

She sat back, pulling her nipple from his mouth, and slid her fingers through the pool of cum. Then she lifted her hand and held it over his face, letting his cum drip down into his mouth.

She slipped her fingers into his mouth, letting him lick them clean.

"We have a lot to clean up, don't we?" she asked.

Later, after she helped him into his chastity device and locked it for him, she kissed him passionately and felt his body surrender to her. She realized how badly he'd wanted to be taken by her and how grateful he was for her having done so.

"You did such a remarkable job making me come, Aaron," she said. "I think I'll be having you serve me on a regular basis."

"Thank you, Mistress Sonia," Aaron replied. "I would," he began, and met her gaze. "I would love that."

"And now you'll need to get back to school, right?" she asked. "I'll arrange for a driver for you. Perhaps I'll make a schedule for you to be picked up and delivered to me. How would you like that?"

"Yes, I mean, I would love nothing more," he replied in earnest. "Thank you, Mistress Sonia."

Chapter 4

On Monday morning, Aaron was walking toward class when he noticed his friend Theo approaching. Theo's silhouette could be identified at some distance since he had a remarkably muscular body. Ordinarily such a well-built male body would have inspired jealousy in Aaron, but he found Theo to be such an incredibly kind person whose generosity precluded such selfish feelings. He wondered if it had anything to do with his having chosen medicine as a field of study. Theo was a nursing student, and Aaron had no difficulty imagining him providing excellent health care to his future patients.

"Hey, Aaron," Theo called out to him.

"Hey," Aaron replied.

"Woah, wait, what's up?" Theo asked.

"What do you mean?" Aaron asked.

"Yeah, don't even try," Theo said, "I can see it all over you."

Aaron gave himself a once-over.

"What?" he asked.

"Oh, come on," Theo said. "You've so clearly been pussy whipped recently."

"Pussy whipped?" Aaron asked.

"Yeah," Theo replied. "You look like you've come up against some really super-dominant pussy that's got you all in a mess."

"Really? You can tell?" Aaron asked.

"Yeah, it's obvious," Theo replied.

"OK, then, I'll admit it," Aaron replied. "I mean, super-dominant is right. This woman is crazy powerful. I can't help but be impressed with myself for having been chosen to serve her."

"Then I am impressed as well," Theo said. "How do you feel about her?" he asked. "I mean, you know, personally."

"She's perfect," Aaron replied.

"That's not really a way that you feel, though," Theo said.

"No, I guess not," Aaron said, "it's hard to say how I feel about her. She's just so impressive. I haven't quite worked out if it's just because I am just really overwhelmed with my respect for her."

"Has she given you any indication of what she wants as far as you're concerned?" Theo asked.

"She had me serve her," Aaron replied. "You know, intimately."

"There you go," Theo said. "Successful submission to a superior."

"And I definitely got the idea that's going to happen a lot going forward," Aaron said. "But OK, what's going on with you? You've been kind of like servant-status with Violet for a while, right?"

"Yeah, but recently it might just be something more," Theo replied.

"Something more?" Aaron asked.

"Like maybe I, well, I don't know. Maybe I love her," Theo said.

"Really?" Aaron asked. "You mean, *love* her?"

"All I can do is think about her," Theo replied. "About serving her. And like your situation, it's hard to say if that's due to my respect for her and nothing less than what she deserves, or what."

"How do you mean?" Aaron asked.

"Well, that's just, you know," Theo said, "sometimes Violet will just want to relieve stress or whatever. She'll have me serve her, sometimes it'll be all afternoon or something. I guess it doesn't necessarily mean she wants more."

"Yeah, I know," Aaron said.

"A number of women have been like that with me, where that's all they want, really, and it might be like that with Violet. Don't get me wrong, I'm not complaining about being given the privilege. But I don't want to overstep in asking for more, you know?"

"Yeah, I completely get that," Aaron said. "You don't want to be annoying. And you don't want to embarrass yourself by mistaking her allowing you to worship her pussy with her wanting you as a personal slave."

"Oh, wow, just the sound of that," Theo said. "Her personal slave. Yeah, I would love to be that for her."

"Maybe you should see if there is a way for you to kind of make it clear to her that you want that, but in a way that doesn't sound like you expect anything from her," Aaron suggested.

"Maybe," Theo replied. "Yeah, I mean, if I see an opportunity to show her that I could be more to her than obedient. More than just my lips and my tongue."

"Well, in the meantime, don't be a fucking idiot," Aaron said, laughing. "Obviously, you'll continue going down on her whenever she wants you to. And as well as you're capable. You definitely don't want to piss her off."

"No, I've made that mistake before," Theo said.

"With her?" Aaron asked.

"No, there was another woman a few years back," Theo replied. "I made the mistake of thinking that because she was having me go down on her that it earned me special privileges."

"Oh, wow, no," Aaron said. "That is a mistake. Just pay tribute to her. Kneel, worship, and remember to show gratitude for the favor she's doing for you in allowing you to serve."

"Yeah," Theo replied. "I learned my lesson."

"Speaking of which, we should get going," Aaron said. "Late to class, bare your ass."

"Right," Theo said. "I should find Violet and see if she needs anything."

※ ※ ※

Violet sat in the atrium of the school's common building, an open, airy space with a small green space in the middle encircled by a short brick wall. She sat on the edge of the red brick wall, which had been worn smooth by age, waiting for her friend Teya. Violet wore a pair of dark-gray slacks, tight about her waist, with a silver belt that appeared as an accoutrement—it certainly wasn't holding up her pants, which would likely require significant force to peel off of her generous hips. Her white blouse made her choice to go without a bra quite evident.

Her eyes seemed to track movement, but not in a frightened or anxious manner, more like someone carefully observing, someone almost detached from the outcome of whatever might be happening around her. She had a nervous tic, though it came off as nonchalance, as she sat coolly swinging a small, thin necklace on her fingers, paying no particular attention to anyone or anything. The small key threaded onto the necklace made a counterweight that swung freely then landed in the palm of her hand.

It was the key to Theo's chastity lock—a recent acquisition. She was thinking about him in an admittedly shallow way, considering his various physical attributes. Theo was one of those boys who looked large, she thought, even heavy, but his hips were so lithe and narrow that they appeared almost delicate. And his hands were like a sculptor's—powerful yet expressive. He had a look of having been out in the sun, almost sleepy yet his chill was due to a relaxed and impatient manner and not a lethargy. He was observant and quick when necessary. His lips were soft and he smiled easily. His eyes were a shade lighter than his skin. And he could do things with his tongue that Violet thought were supernatural.

She noticed a petite woman with long dark hair moving toward her with an energy that suggested she might start skipping at any moment, The thought made Violet smile.

"Hey, hey, hi," Teya said, announcing her appearance. "Whatcha got?"

"Oh. This?" Violet asked in a laconic voice, holding up the key on its chain. "It's a key. On a chain."

"Got that part," Teya said. "Whose?"

"Well, mine, right?" Violet replied.

"Yeah, awesome," Teya said, comically annoyed, "I'm guessing it's to a boy's lock, so I want to know the name of the boy. Is it that one boy, Theo?"

"Yes, it's the key to Theo's lock, if you must know," Violet replied.

"Oh, cool, I like him for you," Teya said. "And I imagine he's coming in fairly handy this time of year."

"That's for certain," Violet said. "The stress of studying for exams without the release I feel having my servant boy go down on me would be, you know. Trash."

"I know, right?" her friend Teya said, pulling her dark, almost-black hair back into a ponytail. "I wouldn't be able to focus in the same way if I didn't have Tyler as my slave."

"You said slave," Violet said.

"Yeah, what?" Teya asked. "He's my slave boy."

"No, that's cool, that's fine, I'm just noting that you said it," Violet replied. "I mean, that's a specific type of arrangement. Are you saying that you've, like, officially taken Tyler as your slave?"

"Yeah," Teya said. "I just decided I liked him, so I explained that he was going to be my slave. Boys are useful, as you know, and Tyler, it turns out, is an excellent fetch boy. So, I presented the choice going forward. He could do whatever I tell him to do, or he could get his ass spanked hard with a paddle, and then do whatever I tell him to do. So far, he's been really obedient."

"That's kind of cute," Violet said. "I haven't found, like, the one boy, you know? I have my servant boy, Theo, but I don't know. Maybe."

"Ugh, I know what you mean," Teya said. "But you've got a lot of boys willing to try, I'm sure. Your crazy sexy body for sure gets them on their knees to start with, obviously, and the whole what-color-are-her-eyes thing."

"That's a thing?" Violet asked, looking amused.

"Isn't it?" Teya asked. "They're, hmm, I'm going to say beguiling. You know that. Like, are they blue, or green, or violet, or maybe gray, like the color of the sky when it's going to rain."

"For fuck's sake, they're blue," Violet replied. "I think."

"Well anyway, they're beautiful in the intimidating way," Teya said. "Which I assume you know."

"I don't really think about it," Violet replied. "I mean, do you actually spend time thinking about your own tight, sexy, perfect little body?"

"Yeah, I actually do," Teya said. "And I am not going to feel any one way or another that I totally get off on myself," she added, laughing. "When I was young, I was really into gymnastics," she said. "It made me really appreciate what having a body like mine could do, you know?

"Yeah, I think that would have been fun for me, but this body wasn't going to let that happen," Violet said, gesturing to her own voluptuous, curvy body and laughing at the thought.

"Well anyway, the thing is, before Tyler became my slave boy, I tried out a number of different boys," Teya said. "I'd let them go so far as to go down on me, but they were never quite right. I'll admit, however, that sometimes there's something hot about their limitations. They just do their best, and I'm just like, keep trying, you know? It just takes them longer. I can't feel bad about that, so I just let them keep at it until I'm finished."

"I know, that's been my experience as well," Violet said. "It's beyond me how a boy can fail at what really should be job one."

Teya laughed.

"Yeah, job one," she said, "that's perfect."

"I mean, Theo is good. He's really good," Violet added. "He definitely has talent. But at the moment, that's all I want from him."

"I totally get that," Teya said. "But at this moment, all I want is lunch."

"All right, then getting lunch is job one," Violet said.

Violet and Teya met up with their friends Serena and Eliana for lunch in the school's cafeteria. The four women were visually dynamic when they were together as a group. Violet was unapologetically dominant and had generously feminine curves; Teya was outwardly and enthusiastically friendly while also being tiny, almost spritely in appearance. Serena had a dark complexion and an almost mystical appearance, and her overtly feminine body appeared as though she willed herself to be shaped that way; Eliana was fair-haired and blond, and she was as innocent and unassuming as she appeared.

Theo and Tyler sat nearby, ready to serve their respective female partners, along with Aaron, who had just become concerned with what he might say regarding his newfound relationship with Ms. Sonia Taylor. He hoped that it wouldn't come up, as he was unsure of what his obligations to her were at this point in time.

During meals, the women had occasion to speak freely, which was a privilege for the boys who were allowed to listen while they themselves ate in silence. The women discussed political issues often, sometimes drilling down on the respective value of certain treaties and economic agreements. They had a confidence in their discourse that the boys couldn't help but admire. Occasionally, the women would discuss the boys themselves, which had the potential of being educational, if not mildly humiliating for the boys to hear.

"The matter is reparations," Serena said. "Ellen Tovald advanced the notion that the price paid in penance for previous misdeeds is not simply a vengeful act, but it is actually a corrective measure in and of itself."

"I'm sorry, did you just say the price paid in penance for previous misdeeds?" Violet asked, over-pronouncing the *P* sound, and laughing. "That's a perfectly presented perception."

"Particularly pleasing!" Teya exclaimed.

"I hate you both so bad," Serena said while smiling broadly. "But my point is that prior to the dissolution of patriarchy, boys had so abused their rights that they were given none in this new, female-dominant society. Now boys don't have any rights aside from those we gift them based on their obedience to female authority. There's a reason for that. And there's cause to assign them reparations."

"You know, sometimes I do feel sorry for boys," Eliana said. "They're born this way, you know? I think it's a matter of recognizing their limitations. They can't be expected to rise to the level of their superiors, by definition."

"I totally get that," Violet said. "Females are socially superior to males, and we have clear biological advantages over them in terms of health, longevity, and resilience, and we're better suited to understanding the social and political transformations that need to take place. But it does kind of make me want to take care of them, you know?"

"Yeah, I feel that they're assigned their station, and as long as they serve well, I want to support them and help them in any way I can," Teya said. "I know they can't handle having the same rights and responsibilities that we do, so I feel an even greater imperative to see to it that they are well-taken care of."

"Now, while I agree with all of that," Serena said, "do I hesitate in the slightest in punishing them when they need it? No. Absolutely not, no one benefits from that. I want them to excel in their position of service to their superiors, but as we all know, boys need correction rather often, and it does them a disservice to deny them that punishment."

Violet picked up her water glass, then noticed that it had no water in it.

"This is empty," Violet said to Theo, holding out her water glass.

"I apologize," Theo said. He took the empty glass and filled it from the water pitcher. He brought it back and noticed that she had a stern look on her face as she studied him. He offered it to her, but she didn't take it right away. Then she simply pointed to its place on the table in front of her. He placed the glass of water, then retreated to his place off to one side of the room.

Dammit, Theo thought.

"OK, take Theo's lapse in being attentive just now," Serena said. "I assume he'll be punished for that?"

"You've assumed correctly," Violet replied. "He's well aware of what his future holds."

"The thing is," Teya said, "I'm unsure if boys are truly capable of the level of obedience we require without corrective punishment."

"I'm all for disciplining the male body," Violet said. "Obviously it's nice to watch a boy getting his butt whipped while he's naked and doing his best to submit. But I agree that I think it unlikely they are even capable of knowing their place without being reminded."

"I have a short leather strap I use to spank boys across the balls," Serena said. "It's always really effective in putting a boy in his place."

"I've always been hesitant about that," Eliana said.

"Oh, don't be," Serena said. "They might not admit it, but they want it. They want the immediate adjustment in their attitude. They will look at you differently, with a deeper respect for your authority. It communicates to them instantly that you don't fuck around. That there will be consequences for any deviation from the path you've assigned them. Believe me, they will respect you for it, and ultimately, they will be grateful."

"So, you just, you know, let 'em have it?" Eliana asked.

"Oh, no, not at all," Serena replied. "No, first I let them know what they've got coming. What their actions have earned them. The anticipation is half of it. They'll feel a kind of dread, and they fixate on it. It will weigh on them."

"Yeah," Teya said, "I've found that the skill, talent, and effort they'll put forth in worshipping me is markedly improved when they have a pending punishment."

"Pending punishment," Violet repeated.

"Oh, shush," Teya said.

"Well, it's certainly true," Eliana said. "They can act silly sometimes. You know, boys. It does serve to straighten them up."

"Most importantly," Serena said, "when I let them know the wait is over, I'll have them beg for it. It's not just their consent that I want, it's an opportunity for them to really express how much they realize they need my correction. Because they do. They all need, want, even crave female guidance and direction."

"Oh, sure, let them know when they've failed and give them the opportunity to admit to it and pay for what they've done," Violet said. "They will do so graciously."

"My slave boy is always so sweet when he asks for it," Teya said. "It's always a really emotional exchange when I let him beg me for a corrective punishment. He's always so sincere and he'll display this profound humility. It's touching, you know?"

Tyler heard Teya's comment regarding his submission to her and it gave him a feeling of pride to be commended by her.

"I do love it when they beg," Eliana said. "But only when I've given them permission."

"Oh, right, of course," Serena said. "Unwarranted begging is the worst offense. That will always, always earn them the strap with me."

"You know, I can't think of males outside of their submissive role," Teya said. "I can't even imagine. I mean, it's the fact that my slave boy is so obedient to my command that really puts me over the edge when he worships my body."

"Yeah, the stress relief of having an obedient tongue is so indispensable," Serena said.

"Yeah, before exams it's critical. And after," Eliana said with a giggle.

"Speaking of exams," Violet said. "We should get to studying."

"Boo," Teya said.

When they'd finished eating, and all of the women in the cafeteria had gotten up to attend smaller meetings or study sessions in variously sized groups, the boys attended to clearing the plates and glasses and table service and then washed the dishes and cleaned the dining room. When the room was spotless and the dishes had been washed and dried, each of the boys attended to their individual obligations.

Some of the boys went around the dormitory to collect laundry. Each of them had been assigned to wash and fold laundry for each of the women, and their schedules were offset to avoid conflict. Some of the boys were assigned to assist with one study group or another, providing service to the women as ordered. Outside of their study groups, boys were also assigned to provide specific tasks such as spa service, providing massage treatment or various pedicure or manicure services. And of course, it was fairly common for many, if not most of the women to relieve stress and relax with a lengthy session of pussy worship with a specific servant, or slave boy.

Chapter 5

"You'll be wanting your punishment now, I imagine," Violet said to Theo later that evening when they were alone in her room. "I know you feel ashamed of yourself for failing in your service to me. A corrective application of the belt would probably feel good right now, is that right?"

"Yes, Miss Violet," Theo replied.

"Then I'm going to have you pull your pants down and get on your knees and elbows. I want to see your bare butt presented up in the air all nice and submissive for me."

"Yes, Miss Violet," he replied as he lowered his pants and assumed the position.

Violet went to her closet and took down the thick strap of leather her mother had given to her as a gift when she left for school. "You'll want this for keeping the boys in line," her mother had said. "Don't be hesitant in its use across the boy's rear end. They don't do well if they're denied the discipline you can provide them. Trust me on that."

Theo had learned to present his ass for punishment in a way that Violet appreciated, a selfless display of full surrender that she found to be more than appropriate. She actually found it touching how respectful Theo was of her authority to punish him. It appeared to her that his entire body was employed in service of offering his bare butt to her to whip with the belt.

"I noticed you talking to Aaron earlier," she said as she sat on the edge of her bed beside where he was positioned on the floor. "What were you two talking about?"

"He said that he had been allowed to be of use to a woman in his neighborhood," Theo explained. "She is a very prominent and powerful individual, and he was surprised to be selected to serve her."

"Interesting," Violet said as she held the belt in one hand and caressed his ass with the other. "Were you jealous?"

"No, Miss Violet," he replied. "I want nothing but to serve you."

"But you do realize that you're just my servant boy, right?" she asked.

"Yes, Miss Violet," he replied.

"To tell you the truth," Violet said, "I kind of like the way that boys would sometimes blush when I've played with them. Like they get a little embarrassed or something."

"Do you want me to be embarrassed?" he asked.

"No, I want you to be however you are," she said. "If having your bare ass up in the air for me to whip with the belt is embarrassing to you, then you would just feel that way naturally."

Violet gently stroked his butt cheek with the smooth leather surface of the belt.

"You know what's funny?" she asked. "It only just now occurred to me that the phrase *bare ass* is in the middle of the word *embarrassed*."

She laughed at the thought.

Then she began whipping him hard across his rear end, bringing the belt down across his naked ass in a consistently relentless rhythm.

"Oh fuck, that's right, Theo," she said while continuing to lash his bare butt with the strap, "take it. Take it hard, submit, and learn your lesson. Show me that you can endure what you deserve."

When she was satisfied that she'd branded his bare ass with an appropriate number of strokes of the belt, she laid it aside and pulled Theo up into a kneeling position.

"Thank you, Violet," he said sincerely.

She smiled and kissed him, sweet and cuddly at first, but soon she seemed to have turned a corner and her kisses had become hot, sexy, and verging on ravenous. In moments she'd taken off her clothes, and Theo was licking her and kissing her body. She held two handfuls of his hair in a playful manner as she rode his tongue and orgasmed several times before she was done with him that evening.

* * *

Theo was, from the moment he met Violet, impressed with her in every way. He'd encountered her at a house party of some mutual friends in the nursing department at school. He had ended up wandering through the house looking for an available bathroom. It was on the lower level of the house where he'd been successful in locating a bathroom that was not in use. The rooms downstairs were lit in a way that his eyes needed to adjust to the darkness, as there were tiny, ineffectual lights placed randomly, and small, curtained windows that admitted meager shafts of moonlight. Theo was on his way back up to the party when Violet appeared out of the darkness.

"Hi, cutie," Violet said. She'd been drinking, and he'd seemingly wandered into her web. "What are you doing down here all alone?" she said as she backed him up against a support beam in the middle of the room.

He'd dressed for the party by wearing a pair of panties and a see-through skirt, and he'd gone topless, as was fairly common for boys at parties. She'd taken advantage of his being naked above the waist to place her hands on his muscular, bare chest in a possessive manner. He responded by dutifully placing his hands behind his back. But it wasn't simply his being well-mannered in an interaction with a female in deferring to her guidance and being obedient to her command; he was immediately attracted to her confidant, even aggressive approach as well as what he saw as her enigmatic and irresistible beauty.

She was wearing a charcoal-gray dress that fit tightly across her extravagantly wide hips and showed the curves of her body to their advantage. Her breasts were prominently displayed such that they appeared ready to burst out of the top, where the neckline revealed her alluringly deep cleavage. The front of her dress showed her soft, feminine belly protruding slightly, with a gentle depression where her navel retreated beneath the fabric. Theo did his best in keeping his eyes level, so as to avoid staring at her figure.

"I was just looking for the bathroom," Theo replied. "And I found it, so mission accomplished."

She placed her hand against the front of his skirt and felt the chrome metal device he had locked around him.

"It's always been a mystery to me how you boys pee when you're wearing these things," Violet said.

Theo tried not to laugh.

"It just means sitting down," he replied. "They're made well, so with a bit of practice, you know. It's not too difficult."

Her hands found the clasp at the waist of his skirt. She gave it a flick, which resulted in his skirt falling to the floor.

"Well, I think you're adorable," she said. "I was going to say you look adorable in your little skirt, but you're not wearing it anymore."

Her hands roamed freely about his mostly naked body as she spoke.

"Now you just look adorable in your little panties," she said.

"Thank you," Theo said. "And you are very beautiful."

"Hmmm," Violet murmured.

He felt the constraint of his chastity cage as he tried not to stare at her magnificent cleavage. Her form-fitting dress was made to display her large round breasts to their advantage, but he'd not been invited to look at her that way. She was curvy, with wide, rounded hips, and she was obviously a bit drunk and definitely horny. She had been become increasingly aggressive in the way that her hands were taking possession of his body. She leaned in and kissed him, pressing him back against the post.

"My pussy is really, um, I have the thickest, fullest bush of, hmm, soft, silky pubic hair," she said.

Theo realized she was a bit more drunk than he'd thought she was.

"Totally natural," she said. "I don't shave it. At all. Like, a wide triangle and super thick and luxurious. You should, um," she said as she looked him in the eyes, "you should see it. Up close. Really close. Don't you think?"

"Yes," he said in a voice that was barely above a whisper.

"No, I don't think you really have an idea what I'm taking about until you see it up close," she said. "It's super thick so you'll have to, you know, your tongue," she said as she placed her hand on his face and slid two fingers between his lips.

He began licking her fingers as she played with his tongue.

"You'll have to use your tongue," she said. "Your face will be right up in my bush. You're so cute in your little panties you're making me all wet. So, it's your own fault, really. My bush will be dripping wet and you've no one to blame but yourself."

He practically swooned as she thrust her fingers into his mouth.

"Oh, fuck," Violet said as she took a step back. "Come here," she said as she led him toward the couch that was against the wall to one side of the room.

Violet pushed him down onto his knees, then sat down and casually put one leg up on the arm of the sofa. The repositioning of her legs caused her short, form-fitting dress to ride up over her hips, to which Violet paid no attention. Theo noticed that she was not wearing underwear. She had a thick dark triangle of soft, bushy pubic hair, and she was entirely unselfconscious about being exposed. Having revealed her naked pussy, she appeared as though she simply wanted him to be aware of her power to confront him with her sex, and that she was supremely confident that he would do whatever she told him to do.

She guided him between her generously proportioned thighs so he could begin licking her pussy. He was impressed with the fact that she had been modest in her own appraisal of how soft and thick her bush was as she brought his face between her legs. She had also underestimated how wet she'd become while talking to him.

He placed his hands on her hips, and he was surprised to feel how extravagantly proportioned they were. His hands felt like they were farther apart in holding her by the hips than he had expected, which made his chastity cage feel even tighter than it already felt. He kissed her gently along her inner thighs, then he began to lick her slowly between her labia, with his face deep in her bush of soft, dark pubic hair.

"That's perfect," she said.

"You're so good at this," she said as she relaxed into the soft sofa cushions. "Let's find out how good . . ." she said, trailing off as she felt each wave of pleasure surge through her body.

He held her tightly by the hips, sensing that she wanted him to be fairly aggressive in pleasuring her body. In spite of his modest experience, Theo had never had a woman be so aggressive in forcing his face into her bush and his lips and tongue into service of her pussy. She was loud as well, gripping him tightly and pulling his hair as her hips began to buck against his face. And finally, he'd never experienced a woman who would squirt when she'd come. She soaked his face, squirting into his mouth the moment her orgasm climaxed, then she had her second orgasm with his head clamped tightly between her thighs.

"Fuck," she said in a soft, breathy voice. "Let me feel your tongue deep inside my pussy. As deep as you can go."

He extended his tongue as far inside of her as he was capable, as though he was fucking her slowly with his tongue.

"Deeper," she said. She placed both hands on the back of his head and pressed his face against her body. She spread her legs further apart and placed both of her feet on his lower back.

After some time, she redirected his tongue to her clitoris. He licked her until she had her third orgasm, which caused her hips to buck against his face, raising up off of the sofa while her feet pressed against his lower back for leverage. She held him by the back of his head to keep his tongue right where she wanted it. When she'd finished coming, she pushed him back onto the floor and straddled his body. She crawled forward and sat on his face.

"Now I want to ride your tongue," she said.

Violet placed one hand on his head, and the other she placed behind her back to wrap around his neck. Holding him in place, she began to thrust with her hips. She began riding his lips and tongue.

While she had not been quiet in her reaction to the pleasure she had felt up to this point, she was now moaning and panting much louder as she fucked his mouth.

"Fucking yes," Violet exclaimed repeatedly as she began to come on his face for the fourth time. "Now just kiss it," she said. She remained straddling his face for a length of time at that point, leaning back slightly and propping herself up with her hands behind her on his chest.

"You have no idea how much I like boys who'll just shut the fuck up and do what they're told," she said as she began slowly grinding her pussy against his lips and tongue. "You know, not just obedient like you're supposed to be, but more. I love it when a boy like you tries to impress me."

She slowly rotated her hips in a circular pattern against his face.

"You really do seem to know your place," Violet said. "I like that. I've had lots of boys just like this, and they usually don't really stand out, you know? I'll ride their face and yeah, I'll come in their mouth, but they don't make the effort to really impress me and make it memorable. Then there's you. You're not just a cute face for me to sit on. You're really talented. I bet you can make me come a lot more if I let you try."

She sat up and pinched his nipples, pulling them hard as she began slowly thrusting her hips. Her pussy slid from his chin to the tip of his nose, then reversed direction, going back and forth across his tongue. She pulled hard on his nipples as she began increasing the pace of the thrust of her hips.

After her fifth orgasm she climbed off of him, turned around, and straddled his face again in reverse. He felt overwhelmed by the desire he had for her at the sight of her enormous, perfectly rounded ass. She pressed her thick bush into his face and her asshole against the tip of his nose. Then she leaned forward, rotating her hips to place her clit between his lips while she put her hands on either side of his caged cock.

"Look how cute my asshole is," she said. "Make me come twice more and I'll let you lick it."

Theo made certain to apply himself to the limits of his capabilities, ignoring as well as he was able how sore his tongue had become already.

"I will literally, as well as figuratively, have my ass licked," she said. "And I demand full insertion of the tongue into my asshole, do you understand?"

"Yes," he replied.

"And not just little licks, you know," she said. "That will seriously piss me off. I want full, long, deep strokes of the tongue in my asshole. Your face should be buried in my ass while you worship me. And when you kiss my ass, again both literally and figuratively, you will use your tongue as well. Always start by kissing the rim, just nice, deep, even romantic kisses with your wet tongue. My asshole is perfect, which you will see for yourself, and you should show recognition of that fact. Worship it. Do you understand?"

"Yes," he replied.

She felt his lips perfectly mirror her labia in a deep, passionate kiss, his tongue alternately proposing and supplicating to her his desire. His tongue became an avatar of his whole person, expressing his desire, his submission, his offering of obedient service, and his genuflecting worship of her body, her mind, and her soul. She could feel his concept of reality slipping away to delve, to plunge into the fantastical realm of her sexual being. His mouth felt as though it were a conduit for his willingness to surrender to her all that he was able to give her, with the promise to endeavor to go deeper, to give more.

"Fucking fuck," Violet said under her breath.

When they went upstairs, Violet introduced him to her friend Teya.

"He was just worshipping my ass," Violet said. "It was so sweet and nice. I could tell he really embraces his subservient nature. It made me think he might be a good servant. I mean, I'll have to see how he takes a whipping, but he checks out so far."

"What's his name?" Teya asked.

Violet turned to look at him.

"What's your name?" she asked.

"Theo," he replied.

"It's Theo," Violet said to Teya.

"Yeah, hi Theo," Teya said with a friendly smile. "I guess you've already found out a bit about my friend Violet, right?"

"Yes, most definitely," Theo replied, smiling.

"And it sounds as though she finds you acceptable so far," Teya said. "I'm guessing that means you know how to grovel and debase yourself for her amusement."

He thought perhaps Teya was asking the question for her own amusement.

"If that is how you describe it, then I defer to you," he replied.

"Huh," she said. "And how would you describe it?"

"It is a privilege to serve her in every way," he replied.

"Well, that's true," Teya said. "I guess you're one of the clever ones. But I know Violet keeps her boys on a short leash. I'll give you a hint," she said. "Don't just be on your best behavior. She'll demand more, expect more, and she deserves more. You'll see. I look forward to seeing how well you obey."

After that night at the party, Theo was offered many additional opportunities to demonstrate his talent in submission to her. Unlike the night at the party, however, the time he spent in worshipping her pussy wasn't limited in duration the way the first time had been. Instead, she would allow him to serve her pleasure for long, luxurious sessions that would begin in early in the afternoon and stretch until early in the evening. She gave him permission to lick and kiss the entirety of her voluptuously shaped body while she writhed in pleasure from his attentive ministration of his lips and tongue.

He always knew he'd managed to impress her when she would at long last allow him to employ the full length of his tongue in worshipping her asshole. She would present her ass for him on her hands and knees, or she would straddle his face to ride his tongue.

"I so love anal sex," she said appreciatively, using her fingers to play with his outstretched tongue. "You're so good at fucking me in the ass," she said, though he knew that she meant with his tongue alone.

Theo had never met a woman with such an interest in oral sex. Her appetite for pleasure was beyond hedonistic to the point of being insatiable. He was grateful to her not only for the time she allowed him to spend with her physically, but also the time she spent in discussing what it meant to truly worship a woman's body. She would allow him to position himself on his knees, with his arms stretched out before him and his hands and his forehead on the floor. In this genuflecting position, she would provide him with guidance and insight, often about rather specific methods of using his lips and tongue, but also about a wide-ranging number of topics regarding his submission and the female's dominant status. Violet was always generous with her praise when he she felt he deserved it, and an education when she thought he had more to learn.

Chapter 6

"Hey, Violet," Teya said on their way to class the next morning. "I'm going hiking next weekend up to the falls. Want to come along?"

"Can't," Violet replied. "I'm going home for the weekend for family stuff."

"Boo," Teya said. "But OK. I'll think of it as a scouting mission for next time."

"Cool," Violet said.

The following weekend, Violet drove home to meet up with her family, an obligation she didn't mind, in part because she preferred to have her brother, Cary, do her laundry to having her servant Theo do it for her. While Theo had the aptitude to perform the task well enough, she recognized that her brother was more practiced in doing so to her specifications, in addition to which she felt that Theo's time was better spent in more direct, intimate service to her needs.

When she arrived home, her mother was in the garden in the backyard, her father was out doing some shopping, while brother, Cary, was studying in his room.

"Hey, Mom," Violet said as she wandered out back into what she felt was a weirdly extravagant display of plants and flowers her mother had cultivated over the years.

"Violet, honey, you should tell me when you are going to stop by," her mother said as she stood up and shielded her eyes from the sun.

"I did," Violet said. "Yesterday. I called you on the phone and said I'd be home on the weekend."

"Oh," her mother said, her nose scrunching up in a look of confusion. "You did? Well, then, I'm happy to have you home. Your father is off doing some shopping and your brother is studying. I have this tangle of weeds," she said forlornly, looking at her garden.

"Why don't you have Dad doing this?" she asked.

"He has no talent, for one, and I do, but also, it's good for my soul," her mother said.

Violet had been long accustomed to her mother saying that various things were good for her soul.

"While you're here, you should talk to Cary," she said as she bent down to continue her weeding. "He's so focused on his studies, which is good, of course, but he should get out more, if you get my meaning."

Violet's mother often remarked that Cary was a good-looking boy, and that he needed a woman in his life. It was a running theme. For the longest time, Violet had no idea how she could possibly be related to her brother. While she herself had long dark hair and a darker complexion, Cary was fair-haired and light complected. But more importantly, their personalities were different beyond simply being aligned with the expression of their respective gender. As forward and aggressively confidant as Violet was, Cary was shy and almost withdrawn.

She had wondered about it until the day she'd brought it up in conversation with her mother.

"Oh, that's because I had this little fling with a boy I had working for me at the time," her mother said. "Really cute, very submissive. Good in bed and all that. Anyway, I got pregnant, and I decided to have the baby. So that's why Cary looks nothing like you."

"Oh, wow, mystery solved," Violet said.

Violet had never felt annoyed with her little brother the way that some women described their relationship with their male siblings. She had always felt that Cary was fairly consistent with his acceptance of his status in relation to her. Her mother had assigned her a position of authority over her little brother from an early age, so she was long accustomed to providing the discipline he needed. She had always been impressed with his behavior, though she felt he needed to be more proactive in offering himself in service to women.

"Whatcha doing?" Violet asked, leaning against the doorframe of Cary's bedroom.

"Oh, hey, Violet," Cary said. "I'm reading a text that explains the historical development of the power dynamic with regard to gender," he replied.

"Oh, that's cool," she replied. "Fascinating subject. You'll learn a lot."

"Speaking of a lot," he said, "it's a lot. I mean it's deep. It's tricky. I'm trying to understand the evolutionary response."

"Well, the way I've understood it in my studies," Violet said, "is that the drive to obey was an evolutionary response to the inevitable transition to a female-led society. The male is driven to obey the female by an innate compulsion that may be mistaken for a sexual urge, when in fact it is simply the biological response to prepare the male to serve its female counterparts. The male body is afforded a reward response for obedience, which assists in making him more pliable and controllable. So that is likely what you're experiencing as a male."

"Yeah, that's what it feels like," Cary replied.

"Boys have always known, somewhere deep in the back of their minds, the true nature of their gender," Violet said, crossing her arms and leaning with her back against the doorway. "Now, many will respond out of fear. They'll act out in defiance of that knowledge, and many will repress it. But once it became culturally acceptable for boys to confess, admit, and express their naturally evolving compulsion to submit to female supremacy, they began to do so in increasing numbers. Eventually, we arrived at our present day in which women are now fully recognized as the superior gender. There is no longer a stigma attached to boys who are open about their drive to be subservient to the female gender."

"Oh, right," Cary replied, though he couldn't imagine there being anything other than an expectation that a boy would openly embrace being subservient to the female gender.

"You know, it was once thought that boys had an inclination toward obedience due to their sexual interest in female dominance," Violet explained. "But that is not actually the case. Rather, it was an evolutionary response to the impending transition to a female-led society. It turns out that the male body has a built-in system to prepare them physically and psychologically to become, essentially, a servant class. The attraction to strong, dominant women is the male body initiating a powerful sexual response, but it isn't sex that the male body ultimately craves. It is female rule. The penis will actually drip in response, as though to lubricate this transition in power. Boys will start to drip this clear fluid when they get excited by being dominated," Violet said, smiling at the thought. "I've seen boys in their chastity locks, naked and kneeling, and they sometimes drip like that. It's the male body simply acknowledging our authority. You can't control it; it's an involuntary admission on your part. Your body actually responds to our authority. Your brain follows."

"But then also, I mean, if I'm not locked, my penis will get hard," Cary said. "Isn't that an admission as well?"

"Yeah, but more so," Violet said. "There's a remarkable correlation between the male compulsion to obey and a resulting erection. It had always been assumed that it was simply the sexual response, but in fact, it was discovered that it is an evolutionary tactic whereby the male body, when confronted with its superior female counterpart, will offer an erection as a survival tactic. It is as though it's attempting to display its usefulness in recognition of the servant position it occupies. Again, it is an involuntary signaling of a submissive status. When the male body recognizes it is in the presence of a member of the dominant female gender, it will display its compliance not as an offering of sex, but an admission or signal of its willing subjugation. And again, the body reacts, and the mind follows."

"So, my penis really does control my brain?" Cary asked.

Violet laughed.

"Well, that is why we ascended to become your rulers, in essence," Violet said. She gave him an empathetic smile. "Boys like you were so badly in need of our control and your physical bodies began to prepare for it long before you even realized the depth you'd need to sink to in submission. But, as you now know, you all did eventually assume your rightful place."

Cary chewed his lip.

"I suppose," he said. "I mean, I'm sure you're right."

"Yeah, dumbass," she said, laughing, "of course I'm right. Anyway, what else? Don't tell me that none of the women in the neighborhood have taken you for a servant yet."

"That would be difficult," he replied. "Because, yeah, none of them have."

Cary thought about the slumber party he'd been to a few months previous, but he decided not to mention it.

"Oh Cary, you fucking loser," she teased, sighing heavily. "You know what you should do is walk your stupid ass over to Isabella's house and like, flat out throw yourself at her feet."

"Isabella?" he asked, not quite able to disguise his wariness. "The woman with," he began, then paused. He realized he shouldn't say *enormous breasts*. He also didn't want to say anything else related to her extravagantly curvy body shape, as that would only serve to objectify her body in what might sound as though he was being judgmental about her overtly feminine figure.

"Yes?" his sister asked.

"With the reputation for being, you know, demanding?" he asked.

"I guess, I mean, what woman isn't?" she asked. "We want what we want, why would you expect anything different? Are you scared?"

"A little," he lied.

She laughed.

"Why, do you think you'll disobey her?" she asked.

"It's just intimidating," he said. "She's known for . . . did you know that she'll just demand that a boy show her his penis? Like, she's known for doing that."

"So what?" she asked. "Just show her your penis. It's simple enough to comply. Seriously, how can you deny a woman your obedience? That's not a smart choice, and it won't go well for you."

"Yeah," Cary replied softly.

"Like any other woman, she'll decide what you will do for her, right?" his sister asked. "Admit that it would be a good look for you if women knew that you'd been selected to serve Isabella. She has really high standards, so it will speak well of you if it's known that you were deemed acceptable to serve her. Think about your reputation as a servant boy. If women learn that you have a good reputation as a servant boy, they'll be more likely to request that you submit to them," she pointed out.

"Request?" he asked. "Surely you mean demand."

"For *you* it will be a demand," Violet said. "See it as the amazing opportunity it is for you as a boy to fulfill your potential in service to your female superiors in general, and maybe a specific female in particular. I mean, come on. Be sharp, be on point, and if one of the women takes notice, which they'll be sure to do if you just project a strong, confident submission to her authority, then she will likely take you aside for specific instruction. That would be a marvelous opportunity for a boy like you to be singled out for guidance. Trust me, women are so giving in educating boys like you. If they see that you have the potential to learn your lessons, remain in your place, and be grateful, they'll be far more interested in determining what other talents you possess."

"Yes, thank you, Violet," Cary replied.

"Anyway, you should make sure to offer yourself to Isabella," she said.

"You're right, I've just been scared," Cary admitted. "I'm sorry."

"Being afraid is just a natural reaction to your superiors," she said. "But it's not an excuse. And don't apologize to me, apologize to Isabella. At least offer yourself to her."

"Thank you, Violet," Cary replied.

"Oh, by the way, my laundry is in the back of my car," she said.

"Oh, thank you for telling me," he replied. "I'll get to it as soon as I am able."

"I know you will," she said with a warm smile as she left him to finish his homework.

* * *

Cary felt nervous while walking over to Isabella's house later that day. Isabella had an established reputation for being cruel to boys who weren't exceptionally submissive, and even boys who did recognize and respect her superiority in the way she demanded were susceptible to her judgement. She was intolerant of boys being disobedient to say the least. His behavior toward her was going to be examined closely, and if she felt it was wanting of correction, she would deliver that correction immediately and without hesitation.

He knocked on the door of her house, hoping that he did not disturb her by interrupting something she was doing. He needed her to be in a good mood to begin with. The door opened, and in that moment, Cary did his best to keep his eyes level with hers. She was wearing a black T-shirt with white lettering across her breasts that read "BOYS SUCK" in a large font type, with the words "MY CLIT" in smaller letters underneath. Her shirt fit the dynamic curves of her body in way that celebrated the overtly feminine shape of her body, and the short, pleated skirt underneath made it appear that she was humorously subverting the implied innocence of the school uniform.

She confronted Cary, staring at him with a look bordering on contempt, and gave her long, wavy, light-brown hair a toss of her head. She fixed her dark brown eyes on him, seeming to pierce him with the intensity of her natural beauty and effortlessly dominant nature.

"Hi, what do you want?" Isabella demanded.

Not off to a good start, Cary thought.

"Hello, Isabella," he said, "I've come to apologize to you."

She examined him.

"Apologize," she said, as though savoring the word in her mouth. "I see. Come in."

He followed her into the house, trying to suppress the feeling that his stomach was tying itself into knots.

"OK," she said as she took a seat on an armchair in a room downstairs. "Stand there. And I'll listen to your apology as long as you make it worth my while.

She examined him, standing before her.

"You're trembling. Are you afraid of me?" she asked.

"Yes, Miss Isabella," he replied. "I admit to having been afraid of what you might do to me. And I admit that I am still afraid."

"Hmmm," she murmured. "Good. I like that. I think boys should be afraid."

He tried his best to remain calm, but Isabella was well-practiced in dominating naked boys like Cary. She could easily determine the level of terror she inspired when they surrendered to her.

"The thing is, Cary, you're right to be afraid of me," she said. "I like to humiliate boys. I like to punish their balls. And knowing that you'll have to show submission to me while I humiliate you is even better. I admit to being kind of a terror. All the boys are afraid of me, which I love."

Cary's throat went dry, and his upper lip trembled, but he nodded his head to show that he understood.

"You know, ever since the slumber party I've been curious about you," Isabella said.

The slumber party in question had become a topic of conversation such that she did not need to elaborate. There was no doubt about which event she was alluding to. A few months previous there had been a sleepover involving three of the young women in the neighborhood. He had simply been in the right place at the wrong time, though ever after he would question whether it was actually the right place at the right time.

The three young women had gotten to talking about boys and what it might feel like to have a boy go down on them. They had gotten Cary alone to themselves, and they decided he would be a suitable boy with which they could explore the subject.

So, one at a time, each of the three girls had Cary lick her pussy. They were seated at a table in the rec room in the house of one of the young women, and Cary was ordered to get underneath the table. They'd fashioned a leash for him using a length of nylon rope. One at a time, each of the young women would take the leash and lead him into position between her legs. It was his responsibility to slip off their underwear, then get to work trying to make them orgasm.

Each of the three young women had an entirely different set of needs as far as the intensity and pressure of his tongue. He was able to read their bodies and settle into the type of stimulation they wanted. The first wanted light strokes of the tip of his tongue across her clit. The second was too sensitive for that and did not want direct stimulation of her clit but rather she wanted him to lick her clitoral hood. The third wanted his lips and tongue on her clit and for him to be aggressive in both licking and sucking. She kept one hand on the back of his head and bucked against his face when she came.

"So, yeah, I heard all about the famous slumber party," Isabella said. "And ever since, I've been meaning to have you for myself, out of curiosity if nothing else."

"OK, so how about you start by stripping down? I don't really believe an apology from a boy if he doesn't at least offer it naked. So, show me that you're sincere."

She gestured, indicating his clothing, then pointed to the floor. Cary felt his heart racing as he realized the best and only way forward was to take off his clothes as she had demanded. It didn't help matters that his sister, Violet, had known full well that this was the likely outcome of his offering himself to Isabella.

Cary began taking off his clothes as she'd demanded, ending with him standing before her wearing nothing other than his chastity device.

"Hmm," she murmured, slowly examining him. "Your apology now, Cary," she said.

"I'm—" he began.

"Woah, stop," Isabella interrupted. "On your fucking knees, maybe?"

Cary realized it was not a suggestion. He got down on his knees and demonstrated his training by correctly positioning them a shoulder-width apart, with his spine straight and his hands placed behind his back with his wrists crossed.

"Nice," Isabella said. "Boys are more attractive when they're naked and on their knees if they actually feel an appropriate level of fear. Now, I believe you wanted to apologize for something?"

"Yes, Miss Isabella," Cary said. "An apology is owed to you due to the fact that I quite clearly know you, and have known about you for however long, but have failed to present myself or make myself available for your use," he began. "Not that you would have needed me to do so. You are obviously capable of having gotten ahold of me at any time for such service. But a woman of your stature is owed the respect of my having at least made an offer of my service to you as a matter of course. To make reparations for this oversight, I present myself to you now, and express my feelings of shame for having been afraid to do so."

"There's that word again," Isabella said. "Afraid."

She lifted one foot and placed it on the seat of the chair. She wasn't wearing underwear. She began slowly playing with her pussy.

"You know, I can make boys do whatever I want," she said. That's because you have a weakness. It's easy to exploit. I can make your little penis hard, and I can make you want me. Then it's all over for you. You're done for. I have this one boy at school who's one of my little slaves. I cock-tease him mercilessly because I know he wants to lick my pussy really badly."

She laughed at the thought, then paused, observing him.

"How do you feel about that word?" she asked. "Pussy. Mine is perfect, by the way. I get really wet, and I taste really sexy."

She laughed. "I can see that you're thinking about it, aren't you? You're thinking about licking my perfect little pussy. Here, let me help you."

She took her hand from between her legs and presented her fingers, now glistening wet, toward him.

"Crawl," she said. "Crawl forward and taste me."

Cary crawled on his hands and knees toward Isabella and opened his mouth. She pushed her fingers between his lips to let him lick her and taste her. It made his penis hurt in its chastity cage.

"That's right," Isabella said. "That's the reaction I'd expect. You want to lick my pussy so badly, don't you?"

"Yes, Miss Isabella," he replied.

"Ha-ha, fuck you," she said, laughing. "You have to earn it."

She watched him trying not to stare at her naked pussy, which she was displaying right in front of him.

"Hmmm, yeah, I like the way your penis tries to get rock-fucking-hard just looking, just thinking about me," she said. "I've heard that it hurts. Wouldn't know, I don't have a penis, but I've heard it really starts to ache and your balls feel all heavy. Is that true?"

"Yes," Cary replied.

"Too bad, you'll just have to wait for it," she said. "I wonder how you'd take to being made to crawl on your hands and knees on a leash. I bet you'd look good, with your body, all hard and naked, wearing a cute little collar with the leash in my hand.

Come along, little pet," she said with a teasing, playful voice. There was a bright twinkle in her eye. "Such good pets you make, huh? Are you a good boy? Do you want to lap up my pussy, so dripping wet from seeing you crawl obediently on the floor? Fuck yes you do. You can't wait to suck on my clit while I drip into your mouth. I get so wet you'll have to just keep swallowing while I fill up your mouth. You'll love it. I bet it'll make your penis want to get so hard in that little metal cage you're wearing."

She sighed, then emitted a moan that became a frustrated sound.

"Come here," she said. "You're allowed to use your tongue now."

Cary crawled forward and began kissing Isabella's inner thighs, enveloped in the scent of her body as he drew nearer her pussy. He gave her long, luxurious strokes of his tongue on either side of her vulva, then kissed her where he'd licked her. He slid his tongue slowly along the outer, then the inner part of her labia. Then he slipped the tip of his tongue between her dripping wet lips, delving into her pussy before he centered on her clit.

"Perfect," she purred. "Now suck it."

Cary placed his lips around her clit and gently sucked it into his mouth and began circling it with his tongue. The scent and the taste of her pussy filled his senses.

"Oh, fuck yes, like that," she said as he began focusing on her clit.

For the next half an hour, he teased and pleasured her body, using his tongue and his lips in service of her undeniably dominant pussy. After that, he had expected that she would be close to having an orgasm, so he was entirely focused on anticipating her desire. He was prepared for her hips to respond by involuntarily thrusting as she began to come, so he was prepared to move with her to keep his tongue where she wanted it. He was prepared for her powerful thighs to clamp down on either side of his head. But instead, Isabella simply placed her feet on his lower back and held him by the back of his head.

She would sigh, and moan, and she gave him no indication that he wasn't doing exactly what she wanted him to do. What Cary didn't know was that Isabella had an extraordinary ability to restrain herself from having an orgasm any sooner than she wanted to. What gave her the most pleasure was to prolong the experience for as long as she was able. It actually gave her some satisfaction to make a boy feel like he wasn't applying himself sufficiently in worshipping her pussy. She felt it made him more submissive to her if he began to feel that he wasn't working hard enough for her and needed to pay greater attention to her needs. But most important to Isabella was that she enjoyed every moment of having a boy worship her. Eventually, she would allow herself to come, but not before she'd felt that he'd truly given her all that she was deserving of in endurance and effort.

"Fucking hell, Cary," she said in a hoarse whisper, breathing hard, "I'm impressed. You've got some talent."

* * *

"So, how did it go?" Violet asked when Cary returned home that evening.

"Isabella said she was impressed with me," he said. "But she said she wants to see me in a pair of panties because I'm a bitch-boy, and I need to endure a humiliating punishment across the balls."

His sister started laughing.

"Oh, wow," she said, "I suppose that means it went well. So let me guess. You were wary of her at first, but now you're terrified."

"Yes," he replied.

"But she didn't do anything?" she asked. "I mean, she didn't punish you yet?"

"No, not yet," he replied.

"Why not?" she asked.

"She said I have to earn it," he replied.

"Oh, right," she said. "You have to show her you can submit to her the way she feels she deserves. And she probably wants the anticipation to be like a torture for you. It's like a test of your self-discipline. It's going to be your fear that she wants to see.

She'll want to see that you're terrified of her, but that you obey her, nonetheless. OK?"

"I guess," he said.

"You guess?" she asked. "Are you doubting me?"

"No, I'm not doubting you," he said.

"Good," she said, "because that would be dumb. When you offer your full compliance to Isabella, think of it as a woman teaching you a lesson. That way you will remember to show gratitude to her for having given you an education in learning to submit to her. Lesson two, keep in mind that she'll want to see your reaction. She'll want to see the expression on your face. She wants to see the humiliation you are feeling in the moment. It will be a little victory for her if she's really taken you down. Let her see it to help her in celebrating the moment. She's doing you a favor in crushing your little ego, so make sure she knows she's been effective in doing so. You'll want to hear what will most likely be her laughing in celebration of her having put you in your place. Let the sound of her laughter really get to you in that moment. Feel the humiliation and let her see that you recognize her power to compel you to feel that way. Show her how your respect for her is significantly magnified as a result. Realize what a gift it is to you to be put in your place by a woman like Isabella."

"OK, thank you," Cary replied, his voice wavering as he spoke.

"You're welcome, bitch boy," she teased, then started laughing.

Chapter 7

The next day, Violet walked over to the home of Ms. Sonia Taylor, her neighbor, and a woman she'd always looked up to as a mentor. Throughout her childhood, Violet had many such visits with Ms. Taylor, and conversations in which her wealthy older neighbor would confer her wisdom. It had been of inestimable value to Violet while growing up.

"Hello, Miss Violet," Ms. Taylor's butler, Harry, said when he opened the door.

"Hello, Harry," Violet replied with a warm smile.

Seeing Harry always brought back memories of Ms. Taylor making him available for what she called "little exercises." She encouraged a young Violet to practice ordering boys around by having her instruct Harry to perform various tasks. The one she remembered most clearly, due to it causing her to become strangely aroused, was dropping a piece of crumpled up paper on the ground and ordering Harry to pick it up for her.

"Pick that up for me, boy," she'd demand.

He'd dutifully bend down to pick it up and hand it to her only for her to repeat the exercise.

"Now pick it up without using your hands, boy," she'd said.

Violet smiled at Harry as he opened the door wide and stood aside, giving her a deep, respectful bow.

"Why thank you, Harry," she said affectionately as she walked into the house.

Violet was always amused by Sonia's house, which was a mansion, really, and it had the occasional, comically ostentatious touch, such as a fully grown flower garden in the middle of the house, what was essentially a greenhouse located within the walls of her home. Sunlight poured in through the glass roof, and the scent of flowers permeated the majority of her home. It took Violet almost a full minute to reach the mahogany paneled library at the back of the house, where Sonia liked to rest on her days off.

"Violet!" Sonia exclaimed. "So nice to see you. Not often now with you off at the Academy. How have you been?"

"Perfect, I'll say, though I might be exaggerating," Violet replied.

"Well, keep saying it and it will become the truth," Sonia said. "If you'll permit me to say so, you've developed so nicely. Beautiful, really. I imagine the boys are quite literally weak in the knees when they see you?"

"Well thank you," Violet replied, "and sure, I've never seen any hesitation when I've ordered a boy to assume the position."

"I should think not," Sonia said with a twinkle in her eye. "How would you like a cocktail?"

"Not too early for that?" Violet asked.

"My ex-husband asked me that once and I slapped him across the penis," she said. "You're fortunate you haven't got one."

"Well, then a cocktail it is," Violet said with an amused smile.

"Oh, good," Sonia said. "It's some kind of a vodka, peach purée, and champagne type of drink I've put together here. Well, one of my servants did so, but I'll take credit for the inspiration."

She poured a frothy pink liquid from a crystal pitcher into two tall glasses filled with ice.

"So, tell me about school and all of that," Sonia said.

"I don't know if you recall that I'm getting my doctorate in education," Violet said.

"Yes, yes, yes," Sonia said as she handed a drink to Violet and they'd each taken a seat in her living room.

"And so, school's good, and I'm looking forward to the end of the semester, finishing my thesis, all of that," Violet said.

"Excellent," Sonia said. "It seems like a lifetime ago that I was working toward a successful conclusion to my own academic career."

Sonia paused for a moment, seemingly in a revelry within her own mind.

"Oh, so some news about my ex-husband," Sonia said, "though he doesn't deserve the title. As you may know, he was so enamored with his certainty that there should be equality between the genders that he began a little support group for the idea," she said with a wry smile. "Do you remember him?"

"Sort of, not really," Violet replied.

"Funny, that's how I feel sometimes. So anyway, he was hoping, I think, to somehow parlay this little group into a becoming national, perhaps even a global movement. I actually thought it was cute at first. Then it grew old real fast. My attempts to tell him he was making a fool out of himself fell on deaf ears. He was so sure of his being correct in his wrong-headed notions that he only doubled his efforts. It became truly embarrassing. At last, I had no other course but to separate from him. That would have been when you were quite a bit younger," she said, smiling warmly at Violet. "I've just today received a message that he's been detained, and he's being held by law enforcement. I find that to be rather fitting. I had a lovely conversation with a young woman, Officer Daniella Fuerza, I believe. She informed me that he is undergoing a correction to his view of his proper place. Anyway, enough about that immature asshole. I still prefer younger boys, just ones who are a little more grown up."

Violet laughed.

"You're an inspiration to me the way you are committed to a particular age bracket and refuse to settle," Violet said.

"I wonder if it isn't due to their acceptance of their place," Sonia wondered aloud. "When I was your age, boys still had the delusion that there was equality between males and females."

"That's so stupid," Violet said. "How did they even think that?"

"They had a difficult time in recognizing their reality," Sonia replied, "but we corrected them, as you know. It was, for the most part, a beautiful thing to witness. But I much prefer the young boys who've never known anything but female rule."

"I completely understand that," Violet said. "I imagine there were lots of males who had difficulty getting with the program."

"Oh, definitely," Sonia said. "There were any number of boys who didn't get it, of course, but that was to be expected. They were slow to realize what had happened. But the others, the majority, they adjusted so beautifully. Because it came to a tipping point. The ascension of women to a position of authority reached a point where it was no longer a question. We had assumed control, as anyone who had been paying attention would have realized was going to happen. And watching the boys fall in line was a magnificent thing to watch."

"I actually kind of think that would have been satisfying to witness," Violet said. "I mean, as it was happening."

"It was satisfying in a way," Sonia said. "The patriarchy, stripped of its power and compelled to kneel in recognition of its new gynarchic rulers, was astounded by the rapidity of the transition, as well as the overwhelming strength of its opposition. In hindsight, it was obvious. I think of the following visual. If you have a scales representing the balance of power, and each side has an identical copy of, oh, let's say, the planet Mercury, the question is how many small glass marbles will it take to upset this balance?"

"Well, that is a very strange experiment and I'm unsure of how one would do it, but I'm going to say one," Violet replied with a whimsical smile. "One small glass marble."

"Correct," Sonia replied. "One. I mean to illustrate that no one was really paying attention to the true nature of this balance and assumptions were made about how power and influence were allotted. It came as a surprise to many of those who had made such assumptions when this dynamic shifted. They did not see a future when the inevitable ascension of female power would result in our supplanting, replacing, and completely overwhelming the established alignment of interpersonal influence and privilege. Boys who'd never questioned their place in the world found themselves entirely lost in the establishment of a protocol in which they were to surrender authority and submit to reality. Some took it well, making the adjustment beautifully. Some, well, they took a bit longer to accept what had happened. It was great sport to inform those who'd remained clueless and unaware of the totality of the transition. These males had to be brought to their knees, so to speak."

"So to speak?" she asked.

"Well, right, I guess I mean literally made to kneel," she said. "Kneel, serve, and obey."

"Surely even they recognized how the male body is uniquely fitted to the kneeling position," she said. "And how the male mind is so well-attuned to obedience."

"Not at first," she said. "Some, yes, others, it took a while. We had some reeducation to do. There were some evolved boys who were well-positioned to accept their new masters, and we had them as our playthings. It was so much fun for us to explore this new reality we'd built for ourselves. Sure, some women acted out, taking advantage of the situation. But most just took it in stride. We just immediately saw men as boys. Boys who were built to serve. We explained to them all that we expected of them, and they realized it was in their best interest to comply."

"It should have been obvious all along," Violet said.

"Well, it sounds ridiculous now, but female dominance was once considered just a kinky sex fetish," Sonia said. "No one quite realized that it was to be adopted as a normative model. As a rule. Some women did, and some boys, but for the boys it was something they mistakenly thought of as a sexual fantasy as opposed to a comprehensive social dynamic. It turned out that conditioning of the male gender to adapt to female supremacy began with porn and erotica. It was useful in rewiring the male brain to have them look at and read material that would model the correct alignment of authority. The more that boys saw women in a dominant position in the sexual arena, the more obedient they became. They were accustomed to the idea of female power and began to crave it in their daily lives. We saw that once boys began fantasizing about powerful, dominant women, they transitioned quite easily. What we didn't know at the time was that it was a form of reconditioning of the male brain to adapt to gynarchy as a social model."

"So, the more they thought about sexually dominant females, the easier they transitioned to a female-led society?" Violet asked.

"Exactly," Sonia said. "It was a kind of self-radicalizing mind control. They had no idea, but the more they fantasized about it, the more they adapted to submission. At first, however, many boys were under the mistaken impression that their craving for submission to female authority was in some way related to their sex drive. They thought that it was related to their needs as evidenced by their erections. This was shown to be incorrect. Boys feel an overwhelming urge to submit to the female gender because of an evolutionary response. Not all boys felt this at first. The ones who did were simply more highly evolved. The others soon followed, however, and it became something of an avalanche. Those that first identified their urge to submit found that they sank deeper and deeper into submission, and eventually, it was the entirety of the male gender that would come to admit what we have always known: the male gender is meant to serve, not rule. Then there were but a few holdouts, boys who simply could not allow themselves to admit what they already knew."

"What happened with them?" Violet asked.

"Oh, they cried and threw tantrums, basically," Sonia replied. "They needed a hard and heavy hand in reconditioning and rewiring their brains to adapt to submission. Best not to dwell on it. There were iron shackles chained to the walls, and prison sentences for some. Hard labor and severe corporal punishment. Quite nasty. But you, Violet, had the privilege of growing up in a world that had already righted itself, thank fucking god," Sonia said, laughing.

"Yeah, you know, I remember watching these videos when I was younger," Violet said. "They'd have this boy who'd be naked and wearing a chastity device while this woman, I think her name was Vivienne Lee, right?"

"Yes!" Sonia exclaimed, clapping her hands. "The indomitable Vivienne Lee. You know I met her once? She was an inspiration."

"Yeah, she would put these boys through their paces in the videos," Violet said. "Showing submission and stuff. I guess it was educational; we all grew up watching those videos."

"Now, she was adamant that the male orgasm was to be denied," Sonia said. "She was instrumental in promoting our understanding that the male orgasm is an inferior sexual response. We would realize that it should be limited, under the control of female authority, and that it should only be allowed under female supervision and with her permission."

"Right, she kind of modeled how to train a boy using orgasm control," Violet said. "Mostly denial."

"I guess that I'm old school," Sonia said. "I just can't help but want to make a boy come. Maybe it's an indulgence on my part. And maybe it's bad for them, but I've always liked the extremely intimate level of manipulating the male body, forcing it to do what I want. My ex-husband, I'd play a game with him where if he ejaculated, something bad would happen. Like his chores would be made twice as hard, or he'd have a punishment. Then I'd make him come. He'd try so hard not to, but as you know, boys are so easy to control. It would be highly entertaining for me to watch him give in, unable to control himself. I'd stroke his erection with just my index finger. He'd struggle and beg. It was adorable."

"Do you wonder if that had a negative impact on him?" Violet asked.

"It probably did," Sonia admitted with a sigh. "I probably should have followed Vivienne's example more closely. She was always a true believer in a rather forward-thinking model of female domination. She was a bit older, even back then, and she'd get the youngest boys. Questionable even, legally, if you get my meaning. They'd have no idea what they were in for with her. So cute and naive. And then she'd make those videos with them as like a public service kind of thing. But I know she had ulterior motives. She'd play with these boys off-camera, of course. Always a new one. Like I said, she was an inspiration to me and to a generation that followed."

"Yeah, I thought she always looked like she was being so cruel in her treatment of these young, hot boys, but you could tell they were so turned on to submit to her," Violet said. "Like, she was a goddess, you know?"

"Well, she made us see that we are all goddesses in our own way," Sonia said.

"I've often thought it impressive that even before they were assigned their rightful place, there were boys who had already voluntarily accepted it," Violet said.

"It was an act of bravery on the part of some really beautifully evolved boys that they outed themselves as fully submissive to the female gender prior to its adoption by society at large," Sonia said. "They offered themselves up for some rather extreme humiliation in doing so. But they were the first to offer their surrender, voluntarily subjugating themselves to female rule."

"Yeah, I am definitely grateful for that," Violet said. "I understand that even the perception of the male body was different."

"Boys just weren't in the habit of attending to their bodies back then, at least not the way they do now," Sonia said. "But obviously, they learned. Eventually, it was common to see video content where the male was completely naked and locked, and it became the standard to aspire to. The female would be consistent in being dominant and only when he had demonstrated his full compliance and submission to her would she allow him to give her oral sex. The central image became that of a boy going down on the female in the video. The women were no longer expected to be naked in the videos, just the boys who were all locked and obedient, going down on however many women they paired him with."

Violet laughed.

"You're describing it like I haven't seen porn before," she said.

"Oh, of course, I'm just illustrating the difference," Sonia replied. "For one, it used to be not only common, but it was practically required to show the boy ejaculating."

"They'd allow the boy to ejaculate?" Violet asked. "Why?"

"The concept of obedience wasn't very well developed," Sonia replied. "We didn't fully understand the value of denial."

"Would he at least show obedience afterward?" Violet asked.

"You mean lick up his cum?" Sonia asked. "No, it wasn't expected that the boy would do so."

"Gross," Violet said. "The least he could do is clean up after himself."

"They didn't know," Sonia said. "They didn't think about it that way. But when boys stopped seeing the male ejaculate in porn, it stopped being a goal for them, and it helped in transitioning to the focus being on his skill in making the woman come."

"As it should be," Violet said, "I mean, I think it would have been obvious."

"The thing is that there were a lot of things that were sort of backward at the time," Sonia said. "Lots of things changed. Male nudity and their relationship with their bodies became something different. Something new. We know that it's good for boys to be stripped naked—they love it, of course, and it's fun. Boys had been denied objectification, something women had come to loathe, for obvious reasons. But having boys on display in a way they hadn't been before meant that they were more conscious of their bodies. They attended to them more, and the nude look of being smooth and hairless, either shaved or waxed, that became the preferred look. And while the boys removed their body hair, women enjoyed, conversely, not having to shave any more than they wanted to."

"Yeah, I can't imagine it," Violet said. "Either my servant boy having any body hair, or me not having a full bush."

"Something that came about due to our having reorganized the relationship between the genders was that women began to, I don't know, I guess *experiment* is the right word," Sonia said. "We were interested in how we would see the male person as well as the male body. In some ways it became a game of dress up, where women would for no other purpose than entertainment have boys wearing little bits of what had been feminine lingerie. The objectification was part of it, of course. As a result, we began seeing their bodies in tight little panties, shaved smooth and hairless. And then it was also proof of their acceptance of their newly assigned role. It made it more obvious that a boy had acclimated when he would show up in some see-through nothing that clearly revealed that he was wearing panties and thigh-high stockings. Making them wear really tall, high-heeled shoes was fun."

"They do look super-cute like that," Violet said.

"High heels were invented by those of the male gender for them to wear themselves, trying to appear taller," Sonia said. "That was eons ago. Women adopted the look for themselves, but eventually it came around to become a symbol of male submission. They began to wear high-heeled shoes and panties and little skirts as a way to signal their surrender to female rule."

"That totally works for me," Violet said, thinking back to the evening when she met Theo, and what he was wearing at the time. "And if nothing else, it makes their chastity lock more accessible. To check compliance, you know."

"You know, a funny thing is that when I was younger, there were plenty of people who still thought chastity cages or locks were a kinky sex thing," Sonia said. "They didn't understand. They thought it wasn't healthy for the male to have his orgasms controlled. We now know this is the opposite of the truth, and that being locked is one of the first and best things for the male mind and body."

"Yeah, that's weird," she said. "I can't even think of a boy not being locked up."

"Right, but it took some time for that realization to sink in," she said. "And so it wasn't expected for a boy to wear a chastity cage. They'd always had them, and some of the, shall I say, more evolved ones were already wearing them. But then it became customary. Now it is practically mandatory."

"I thought it *was* mandatory," she said.

"Not all women have their boys locked up," she said. "But more importantly, the revelation that was most obvious and most undeniable was that an *owned* penis is superior to any other option. Once it is in the possession of a woman, it becomes something far better than what it was previously. First, it's owned, then, it is obedient."

"Well, hopefully," Violet said. "I've got my servant boy in a really small cage, which I find gives me the control I want."

"Good," Sonia said. "You know, it wasn't until we had a majority of boys locked in chastity that we began to see the results and could no longer deny that this was the best way forward. It was so obviously freeing not only for boys, but for women as well. It used to be that women were very worried about their daughters being around boys. But once they could verify that a boy was properly locked, they were no longer concerned with whatever might happen."

"That was definitely the way with me," Violet said. "I'd have boys over to the house and my mom would absolutely leave us alone after she'd check his lock."

"Right," Sonia said. "Young women could have their boy-toys alone, and the most that would happen is that he would get an education in performing cunnilingus. Which is what happened, of course, and as you know, young women became accustomed to that. Young women began to talk to their friends about which boys were good at it. And that became competitive for the boys, so they stepped up, to their credit. Once their social cache became attached to their skill in bringing a woman to orgasm with their tongues, they quickly adapted."

"That seems like it would have been a definite improvement," Violet said. "Of course, I've never known any different. When I started at the Academy, I wanted to try out a lot of the boys just to find out who was good at what. Speaking of which, I should get going. I need to get back to the dorm tonight to study for a test tomorrow."

Well, it was lovely talking with you as always," Sonia said. "Please feel free to stop by anytime. Oh, and I'm interested in meeting this boy you mentioned," Sonia added. "Theo, I believe?"

"Yeah," Violet replied, "that's my current servant boy."

"Yes, him," Sonia said, "I am interested in seeing this boy of yours. I'm sensing he might be more than just a servant boy."

"Really?" Violet asked. "I mean, sure, but I'm not sure how you've come to think that. That he's something more."

"It's just, oh, I don't know," Sonia said with a curious smile, "I've known you since you were very young. Maybe it's your tone of voice when you've mentioned him. Anyway, it would be nice to have a look for myself."

"I defer to your wisdom, of course," Violet said. "See you next time."

Chapter 8

When Violet returned to her dorm, she had Theo come to her room immediately.

"Did you enjoy your weekend?" he asked.

"I did," she replied. "Clothes off."

"Yes, Violet," he replied, removing his clothing as quickly and efficiently as he was able.

Violet had Theo sit next to her on the sofa in her room and tucked her feet up underneath her as she leaned into him and kissed him, her hand sliding up along Theo's inner thigh. She watched him closely as she closed her hand around his balls.

"You know, it's funny," she said, "I guess I was a bit naive. When I first learned that boys wore a device locked around their cock and balls, I was kind of dismayed thinking it would protect your balls. I didn't know a lot, I guess, but what I did know was that I wanted to be able to have this level of control. I knew that boys were really sensitive here," she said as she pressed his balls between her fingers and the palm of her hand.

"I didn't want a boy to have any kind of protection, obviously," she said." When I first had a boy pull his pants down so I could look at his chastity device, I was really happy to see that they had been really clever in designing it. It locks up your penis, but it leaves your balls completely defenseless."

She smiled at the thought while gripping him more tightly. He groaned softly.

"Shhh," she said. "There's a lot worse coming to you. Show me how big and strong you can be. Show me obedience and self-discipline. Impress me."

She kissed him, pulling his head back while clamping his balls tightly in her grip.

"You may be lesser than me, Theo, but that does not mean that you don't have an important role to fill as my servant," she said.

"Thank you, Violet," he replied. "I love serving you."

"And right now, it would really help me to work off this feeling of aggravation I have if you were to submit to a beating," she said. "I just feel tense and frustrated. I'm probably just worried about the exam I've got coming up."

"I will take a punishment if that is what you want," he replied.

"Of course you will, and yes, that is what I want," she said. "That is very much what I want."

"Yes, Violet," he said. "Should I assume the position now?"

"Yes," she said. "I want you on your hands and knees right here," she said, pointing to the floor before her.

He assumed the position. She placed one hand on his bare ass.

"Hmmm, I'm going to make this hurt," she said. "And I mean really hurt bad. I'm just so on edge, and I want to really beat you hard. Do you think you can take that for me?"

"I will do my best," he replied.

"Oh, I know you will," she said, caressing his butt cheek. "You're always so sweet with your submission to me. Stay in place," she reminded him, though she didn't need to, then she stood up and crossed the room to her closet. She had a long, thin riding crop hanging from a hook on the side of her closet. She lifted it up and carried it back to where Theo was positioned on his hands and knees.

"Your butt is super cute," she said as she sat down on the sofa. She placed the whip against his bare butt cheeks. "I'm going to turn it bright red. Just think about how much I love to see boys obey. Think about how satisfying it is for me to see you offer up your body to me for punishment. And I'll make sure to tell everyone that you took it well. I will be watching you to see how you react to my relentless application of the whip across your bare ass, and I will be sure to tell everyone how well you took it. So, think of it as not just being whipped by me alone. Rather, think of it as everyone watching, like an audience, to see how well you do in enduring your punishment."

Violet brought the riding crop down across his naked ass ten times in quick succession. Theo felt each stroke sear his skin, but he obediently remained in place.

"You know we all talk about it, right?" she asked. "Me and the other women, I mean. When we meet and spend time with any particular boy, and we find him to be remarkable in his ability to follow orders, we are sure to mention it to our friends. Whenever I've given a boy a punishment, of course I'm going to observe closely and judge his reaction and his capacity for enduring what punishment I give him."

Violet gave Theo another ten strokes of the whip, delivered hard, making each of them count. Theo maintained his position but could not restrain himself from emitting a gasp at the sensation of Violet's relentless application of the riding crop.

"And I'm sure to be open with all of the other women; it's information we all want to know," she continued. "I'll say whether or not I think a particular boy took it well, or if he needs better training. It's good for you boys, I think."

Violet unleashed another ten strokes of the whip, focused on the lower curve of Theo's butt, toward the top of his thighs. Theo's jaw clenched tight, and he exhaled quickly, which made a hissing sound. He purposefully got control of himself, steeling his body against the urge to move out of position.

"Last semester I had this one boy who couldn't hold himself still for a beating," Violet said. "It was kind of symbolic of his inability to know his place, you know? It's so important for a boy to learn to remain in position and take every stroke of the whip without squirming around."

Violet brought the whip up, held it for a moment, then delivered another ten strokes in quick succession. Theo felt proud of himself for remaining in place, but he knew the punishment was far from over.

"So anyway, this boy was just so fucking disobedient," she said, shaking her head. "So of course, I told all the other women how he'd behaved when I was giving him what he deserved. I made it public knowledge. The result was that all of the women in my dorm made a point of taking this boy aside for some individual attention. We all took a turn with this boy. He had his pants down for punishment constantly throughout the fall and spring semester."

Violet gave Theo another ten strokes of the whip, during which he felt his adoration of her deepen, and the pain that she delivered intensified his respect for her.

"By the end of the year, I was hearing that he'd learned his lesson," Violet said. "He'd become a magnificent example of a boy that could not only take what he had coming to him, but also display endurance and gratitude. Which is what I expect from you, Theo."

She gave him another ten strokes of the whip, but delivered them slowly, one at a time, each harder than what had come before. Theo made several involuntary gasps, almost a whimpering sound, but otherwise he was able to maintain control of his body while she whipped him.

"As I am sure you are aware, I am very appreciative of obedient cock," she said. "It's clearly a higher purpose for you to serve and surrender to the female gender in any way that you can. And I think you have potential. I will admit that it's crossed my mind to take you to be my slave."

Violet repeated the ten strokes delivered individually and methodically, pausing after each one. Theo heard her say the words *be my slave,* and he felt them being branded into his ass by her whip. It served to help him recommit to enduring the pain of her whip.

"I'd like you to test you in a number of ways first," she said. "I would love to see how well you'd take a month of hard submission. Ball-gagged and wearing some really tight, restrictive bondage, locked, of course, and receiving daily punishment while serving me. That would be fun to watch. I bet you'd do fairly well."

Theo took her words as the compliment she'd intended, and the next ten strokes of the whip made him feel a gratitude beyond anything he'd felt before.

Violet put the riding crop aside and placed her hand on his left butt cheek, feeling the heat rising from his skin.

"You're such a good boy, Theo," she said softly. "I'm impressed with how well you took your punishment."

"Thank you, Violet," he replied, his profound respect for her apparent in his voice.

* * *

"How was the visit back home?" Teya asked Violet when they met up the next morning.

"Cool, cool," she replied. "Saw my family, met with my neighbor who's kind of a mentor to me."

"So hey," Teya said, "we should stop over at Serena's room. There's a live feed of the interrogation of that boy, you know who I'm talking about? He was an opponent of female supremacy who'd attempted to mount a campaign in support of maintaining gender equality. You know, what's-his-face, um—"

"Charlie Taylor," Violet said. "Or at least that was his married name. I don't know what it is now. Coincidentally, he is the ex-husband of the neighbor I was talking about."

"Oh, wow. That's surprising," Teya said. "So do you know him?"

"No, not really," Violet said. "Only through stories, really."

When they'd gotten situated in Serena's room, they logged onto the police website. In interest of transparency in policing, video from all interrogations were streamed live and then archived on their website. The video was presented without audio in the interest of maintaining secrecy in an investigation, but viewable by the public as proof that all interrogations were conducted in a lawful manner.

After what the four women deemed an unreasonable length of time for them to have to wait, Charlie was brought into the interrogation room.

"Ha!" Serena exclaimed. "There's the fucker. Appropriately outfitted, I see."

Charlie was handcuffed and locked in chastity, but otherwise naked, as per the standard protocol for male inmates. A unique aspect of the chastity lock he'd been fitted with by law enforcement was a coupling on the bottom of the base ring that attached to a vertical metal rod in the center of the interrogation room. Charlie was made to stand straddling the vertical metal rod, then bend his knees just enough to attach his chastity device to the rod, which then effectively held him in place.

"I wish they had accompanying audio," Teya said. "I'd like to hear what they say to him."

"Apparently it's for when they don't want to give away any details in an investigation," Violet said.

"I like the inverted chastity lock that the cops use," Serena said.

"They look so tiny and cute," Teya agreed. "I like boys who have a teeny tiny penis. Like my boy, Tyler. He's super cute and tiny. It means he can wear the smallest, most restrictive chastity lock, which makes me crazy. I get so turned on just seeing that tight little cage on his penis."

"OK, but would you rather a spiked cage or an inverted one?" Serena asked. "I assume that we all have a preference."

"I like the inverted design," Teya said. "Flat-out denial, so his penis doesn't even have an opportunity to get hard."

"I don't disagree with the motivation," Serena said, "but there's something deliciously devious about the spiked cage. It allows him to get just a tiny bit aroused, but if he does, he'll regret it. I like the option, so that he comes to realize that he is free to become sexually aroused, but it's going to hurt." Serena laughed in a mean-spirited way, thinking about the sharp metal spikes on the cock cage pressing against the shaft and the head of the penis. "I know he can't help but get not hard, but harder, when I straddle his face. In reverse, so I can watch it happen."

"I know this is not the norm," Eliana said, but I actually like the whole straddle in reverse thing that Serena mentioned, but I'll have a boy unlocked. That way I can see the full expression of his arousal."

"Aren't you concerned that he might inadvertently ejaculate?" Teya asked.

"It's not like he hasn't been warned, so I've got the strap in hand," Eliana said.

"Of course, you can have a boy however you like," Serena said. "But ideally, boys should want to be caged, locked up, and denied. Obviously. They should want their penis locked up so that they can focus their attention. Boys who don't want that simply lack maturity. Think about it. A young boy will want to have a toy to play with. But at some point, he will put his toys away. Why? Focus. He knows that the attention given his task is of primary importance. That's a mark of maturity, when a boy voluntarily puts his toys away to focus his attention on what is of greater importance."

"That actually makes a lot of sense," Eliana said.

"Right," Serena replied. "The male who has grown to maturity will want his penis locked up because he knows that the attention given to his task will be greatly increased, so that he will not be distracted. When he kneels in pussy worship, his mind will have no other thought but that of providing pleasure. His attention should be entirely on the woman's body, and he will want to be locked in chastity for the duration."

"Forgive me if I'm slow to get a handle on this, but what did this boy do again?" Eliana asked, indicating Charlie on the live feed from the interrogation room.

"Apparently," Violet said, "he was out driving after curfew. He was stopped by the police and taken into custody, of course, to find out what he was doing, if he's hiding anything, et cetera. Turns out that he's one of the last of the resistance to female supremacy. He was a prominent voice in the gender equality movement, which had attempted to resist female authority on the belief that boys are equally suited to holding power."

Eliana's mouth fell open while Serena and Teya both laughed.

At some point in the interrogation, the police officer attending the interrogation inserted a ball gag into Charlie's mouth.

"Oh, I guess they've heard enough," Teya said.

"Yeah, too much boy-talking, apparently," Violet said, chuckling at the sight of Charlie being silenced.

"That's when the ball gag is mandatory," Serena said.

"Absolutely mandatory," Teya agreed. "I don't like boys who think they should talk when they haven't been directly asked for input. Any of the boys in my life will end up wearing a ball gag at some point."

"I find that even the most well-trained boys will speak out of turn," Serena said.

"The ones I like most are the boys who know their place, and I strap the ball gag on just because they look so cute wearing it," Teya said, laughing.

"I bet my servant, Theo, would look attractive wearing a ball gag," Violet said. "I'd love to see him wearing one. And nothing else, of course."

The police officer on the video feed had repositioned Charlie with his hands raised up behind him by a steel cable, forcing his body into an awkward position. Then she acquired a tawse, which she was clearly intending to use across Charlie's naked body.

"Ooh, he's going to get it now," Serena said with obvious pleasure.

"Yeah, she's so boss," Teya said. "She looks like she means business. If I was a boy, I'd be terrified of her."

The four women watched as the officer began to whip Charlie, and they were impressed with how relentless she was in punishing him.

"I can't imagine how humiliating it must be for him," Eliana said, "getting his punishment on a public website."

"He clearly deserves it, so it's good for him," Serena said. "He'll be grateful for it in the end, I'm sure."

Suddenly the video feed from the police department's interrogation room went dark.

"Oh, boo," Teya said. "Also, what the fuck, we were enjoying that."

Chapter 9

It had been almost a decade since Charlie met and began dating Sonia Taylor. He was entranced by her aura of power and self-determination, and he found her to be extraordinarily beautiful as well. He would eventually become her husband, but long before that, he realized that he was going to need to be on his best behavior to have a relationship with her. He did his best in being respectful, well-mannered, and consistent in deferring to her on every issue and following her lead. But he occasionally felt it unfair to be expected to submit to her in such a comprehensive and even intimate manner. She wanted him to obey as a matter of practice on a perpetual basis, in addition to his submission to her sexual dominance.

His interest in promoting gender equality was something that Sonia first found charming, even harmless. She allowed him to express his thoughts on the matter, but he soon came to realize she was just humoring him and expected him to remain fully submissive to her regardless.

"I think you've taken this all a bit too far, Charlie," Sonia said at last. "I thought it was cute, if not a bit pathetic, but now it has become irritating."

"Irritating?" he asked. "Seriously, you're irritated about my wanting men to be seen as equal to females of the same age and station in life?"

"I don't like your tone of voice," she said coolly, "and what you are saying is patently ridiculous. Boys should in no way be considered equal to women. Pants down. Now."

Sonia retrieved a thick wooden paddle while Charlie complied with her order, lowering his pants and assuming the position to receive his punishment. She paddled him, one of many such attempts to correct his behavior, but he continued to hold onto his beliefs regarding gender equality. And over time, his conviction in upholding these beliefs would deepen, and though he took his punishment, it would turn out to be the last he would agree to endure.

Finally, Sonia decided that he was beyond saving, and she filed for divorce. His paychecks were still deposited directly to her bank account, which he found particularly painful because she was independently wealthy. She didn't need his money, but their marriage had made the transfer of his money to her irreversible. She made the allowance that he was still offered the privilege of driving one of her cars, and she didn't avail herself of the various humiliating public punishments she had a legal right to assign him as a result of the divorce.

But Charlie continued with his campaign to try to raise awareness of the issue of gender equality, which would end the moment he was pulled over while driving after curfew by Officer Fuerza.

* * *

Charlie was brought into the interrogation room by Officer Daniella Fuerza and two additional officers, whose job it was to observe. He wore handcuffs behind his back, the chastity lock he'd been assigned, and nothing else. Daniella attached his chastity device to a vertical metal rod in the center of the room, which held him in a position that was not quite squatting, but less than standing up straight. It was an awkward position for Charlie, who felt humiliated to be displayed almost entirely naked. He was keenly aware that the camera on the wall was streaming a live feed on the law enforcement website.

"You know, I'm interested," Daniella said, "tell me, because I am just so fascinated why you think your gender is equivalent my own."

He had a sour look in response.

"No, no, don't get that look on your face, that's surely not going to help. Chin up," she said, lifting his face up with her fingertips. "Come on, show me your equality. Smile, maybe? What do think, shouldn't he give us a pretty smile?" she said to the other women in the room.

They chuckled.

"Maybe he should stand up straight, what do you think?" she asked aloud. "It wouldn't hurt to show respect, right?"

He grimaced at the thought since he was already feeling the restraint on his balls. Daniella laughed.

"Now be brave, and strong, and explain your right to be considered my equal," she said.

Charlie's brow furrowed. He decided to make his case, thinking that he hadn't anything to lose at this point.

"Well, for one, it should be unconstitutional to discriminate on the basis of sex in the workplace," he began. "I believe that all genders ought to be treated as equals in every situation. Women should at least recognize and fully accept that they are given gender privilege, listen to men who voice their oppression within the gynarchical system, and use their privilege to benefit those who do not share that privilege. Because women are in a position of greater social power, men are systematically discriminated against, to the point that they are treated as subordinate or otherwise less than the dominant female gender. Men are culturally, socially, and legally considered lesser beings."

Daniella had a look of amusement on her face as she listened.

"Women need to be reminded of their own privilege," Charlie continued. "Being in a position of greater privilege as women, they don't seem to realize how much less the men at her workplace make, or what it's like to have women dismiss their opinions or interrupt them on a regular basis. And the expectation of sexual, or bodily submission, I mean, how can you not realize the impact of having me here, bound by my genitalia for fuck's sake? And otherwise naked, to be displayed publicly through the law enforcement website?"

"All right, that's enough, Charlie," Officer Fuerza said. She walked around to stand behind him and brought a ball gag up and around his head and held it in front of his face. "Open your mouth," she said.

She said it in a tone of voice that made clear that obedience to her command was his only option.

"Good boy," she said as she inserted the ball gag into his mouth and pulled the straps tight, buckling them behind his head. "Perfect. Now you will shut the fuck up and listen. You should become accustomed to being silent when a woman speaks."

She walked around to stand before him.

"Do you want me to break it down for you?" she asked. "Do you need me to explain it to you? I'm not asking to be mean; I sincerely empathize with your situation. I'm sure that it must be confusing for you. Your gender simply isn't built for this level of understanding. You've come up against a very complex set of ideas and you have, in essence, gotten tripped up. Believe me, I understand. I'm sure it looks quite complicated from where you stand. If that's what you call standing," she said with a smirk, glancing down at his posture.

Her remark caused Charlie to feel a rush of humiliation, which surprised him as he thought he couldn't feel any more humiliated than he already was.

"This is why women have boys kneel," Daniella explained. "Because it can be very simple. You just need to accept that these very complex issues are, in fact, fully understood, it's just not for you to understand them. If you surrender and assume your natural place in the world, you will know a profoundly peaceful existence. Those of the female gender will take full responsibility for your well-being. We offer this to you as a gift. All we require of you is your full commitment to serve. That's it," she said, cocking her head to one side. "All you have to do is submit, obey, and surrender to us, and we will see to it that you will be taken care of. We so appreciate boys when you offer service to us in our quest to make a better world for all of us. Rid yourself of distracting thoughts of your own desire. Give in and become a useful servant to the superior gender. It will be so rewarding to you."

Daniella stood with her arms crossed as she considered Charlie, someone whose beliefs she had no sympathy with, but whose potential she thought she might be able to have a positive effect in promoting.

"You're just making it hard for yourself," she said. "All you have to do is give in. Give up. Surrender. You been beaten. Admit it. You can't compete, you can't win. You only have one choice, which is to recognize what is so clearly right in front of you. Your gender tried and failed. You lost. Accept it. You're a male, and the male gender is inferior to the female gender. In your daily life, you will need to learn to say it. Say it out loud and admit your defeat. We won't hold it against you that you made the mistake of thinking you are our equal. We understand your limitations. We just need you to become aware of them. We need you to admit to being the least qualified to make decisions about what you should do. Women are far, far better at making those decisions for you. All you need to do is follow directions. Can you do that, Charlie? Can you follow directions? Because you will need to do that. You will need to begin by admitting your mistake in thinking you are our equal, and then agree that your best and only option going forward is to obey. Listen to women when they tell you what to do and obey their command. It's easy once you give in. Once you surrender."

She then attached an aluminum carabiner to his handcuffs, which in turn was attached to a steel cable that ran from its point of connection on the ceiling to where his handcuffs were raised up behind him. His arms were now held extended out and just below shoulder level. He winced at the discomfort of being forced into such an awkward position,

"In the meantime, you are assuredly experiencing something that is a result of an evolutionary development," Daniella explained. "It is in response to the establishment of female authority. The male body responds to the dominant female by what we have identified as biological submission. This is where the male body itself begins to recognize an absence of discipline by way of physical punishment. Where the male has properly subjugated himself to female rule and consistently displays an obedient response, this bodily response does not manifest in an appreciable way. However, when the male in question begins to show deviant urges in acting out, and failing in his obligation to obey, any lack of commensurate punishment will be keenly felt by the male body. It will gnaw at him like a hunger, driving a compulsion to submit to punishment. You've likely felt this, have you not, Charlie?"

He felt a new wave of humiliation, now due to his realization that what she was saying was correct. He did feel absent the catharsis of corrective punishment as uniquely delivered by a dominant female.

"The male brain may not be in alignment in any given moment," she continued, "which may lead to some confusion on his part. But his physical body will be quite certain of its needs, and it will cause the male to seek out correction. The male body will simply crave this response. When boys are not attended to and provided discipline, they behave poorly. So law enforcement is occasionally saddled with this duty to punish the male body."

Daniella held an implement in her hand, which she presented to Charlie for his examination.

"This is a tawse," she said, "an implement of Scottish origin, long used in corporal punishment. This particular one is new, very stiff, and freshly oiled so as to provide an unforgiving sting to the welt it will leave on your bare skin. You may not enjoy the sensation, but you will come to appreciate how effective it is in delivering the corrective punishment you so deserve."

She then began to use the tawse in whipping Charlie across his bare ass, then across his chest. She went back and forth, torturing him with an alternating forehand and backhand stroke of the implement across his naked body.

"Keep in mind, Charlie," she said as she punished him, "you're only getting what you deserve. You've failed to assume your rightful place, and you need to be shown how wrong you are in thinking you're anything more than the servant class you've been assigned."

She punctuated her message with hard strokes of the leather straps across his exposed skin, raising pale pink welts where she landed each swing of the tawse. Charlie felt each painful, humiliating stroke, and issued an agonized groan that was muffled by the ball gag strapped tightly around his head.

"Far better of your kind has willingly surrendered," she said, "showing humility in defeat and bowing before their betters. But you? You're just an embarrassment, Charlie. Your failure to recognize your place in submission to those who are so clearly your superiors is shameful, really."

She introduced the tawse across his upper back and his thighs, now ranging across his body such that he was never certain where the whip would land next.

"I'm only giving you precisely what you have earned for yourself, in hopes that you show the capacity for learning your lesson. The lesson is, of course, that you've only one choice, and that is to offer up your full submission. You will learn to submit to me, and all of the women you encounter for the rest of your life. You will accept your position as servant to female authority, and you will do so graciously. You will openly admit to having been corrected in your estimation of your own status. You will recognize your rightful place in submission to your female superiors."

By the time that Daniella had concluded her lecture, Charlie was marked with blushing crimson stripes across his chest, his ass, his upper back, and across the front and back of his thighs. He had tears in the corners of his eyes and his head hung in surrender to the waves of humiliation and pain coursing through him. But he felt something else as well, something he'd not anticipated. He felt a begrudging respect for Officer Fuerza.

She'd beaten him in such a comprehensive and effective manner, delivering the shaming she'd felt he deserved in a way that had gotten to him and made him question his view of himself. What he hadn't anticipated was that if not for the inverted chastity lock on his penis, he would have become fully erect during the beating the officer had given him. It made him feel grateful to have been locked up so completely, as an erection would have signaled a confession on his part that he was unwilling to admit to at this point.

After he'd been taken back to his cell, he lowered himself gingerly onto the bed, feeling the sting of the tawse reverberating through his body as well as a soreness in his jaw from having worn the ball gag. The device on his penis still felt tight from his body's attempt at having an erection. It occurred to him to wonder who had been watching the law enforcement's website live feed of his interrogation and punishment. He wondered if his ex-wife Sonia had seen it and imagined that she would have taken great pleasure at the sight of him being punished. He experienced a deepening of his feeling of humiliation at the thought, but his own mind suddenly turned traitor as the memory of licking her pussy came to mind. There was a coinciding rush of feelings, contradictory to one another and confusing. He longed for her in a way that he hadn't in years.

Chapter 10

When Officer Daniella Fuerza returned home that evening, she was in a mood. Having spent a part of her day lecturing and punishing Charlie, she was on edge, having no tolerance for anything but total submission from her slave-husband. Luckily for Tom, he'd attended to his domestic chores that day with better-than-average results, which left their home in exquisite order.

"I am impressed with your work," Daniella said as she walked in the front door and surveyed the state of her home.

"Thank you, Master," Tom replied, having assumed the kneeling position in anticipation of her arrival.

"You've been well-trained, which is one of the most attractive attributes of a slave-husband," Daniella said, then leaned down to kiss him.

Tom felt grateful that he'd been raised in such a way that he'd learned a great deal about domestic upkeep. His mother assigned him the entirety of the chores around the house when he was young. At the time he'd resented the fact that he was given the responsibility of cleaning and doing the laundry while his two sisters were free to do as they pleased. He'd made the mistake of grumbling about it on more than one occasion.

"Oh, whatever," his sister said, "I mean, sorry, not sorry, that's just the reality of your gender. If you have a problem with that, then don't complain to me. I'm not the one who made your gender a servant class. Do you need a correction of your attitude?"

"No, I apologize for complaining," he replied.

"So, you admit that you were complaining?" she asked. "I guess you do need some time to think about your obligations, don't you? And if you felt the sting of the belt across your bare butt, you just might come to have the appropriate outlook on your place in the world. Your gender is best relegated to a servile position, and complaining about is not just immature, it's embarrassing."

Tom ended up with his rear end a uniform crimson that afternoon, and he did come to feel grateful for having been corrected on the matter. As a direct result he focused on the task of scrubbing the floors and sanitizing the bathroom and kitchen and vacuuming and dusting the home until it was impeccably clean and orderly.

When Tom had first moved in with Daniella, he noticed that she had was a plaque on the wall that read "Denial, Discipline, and Domestic service."

"The three Ds," Daniella said. "My tits are double Ds, but my boys are all triple Ds." She laughed, then added, "Seriously, though, it's there as a reminder. When you've got a pair of blue balls and a bright-red butt while you're scrubbing my floors, just remember that you're exactly as you should be. If your balls ache and your butt stings and you've got bruises on your knees, then you're probably providing excellent service. I just enjoy the benefits. Why would I not? I need you focused on me at all times, Tom, ready to serve. You will need to pay attention, and I expect you to learn what I will want of you at any moment such that you come to anticipate my desire. Eventually I will expect that when I open my hand, you will have already acquired for me that which I wish to have placed in my hand at that moment. Sometimes it will be very simple. Like now, for instance. I want you to place your balls in my hand."

Tom stood and placed his balls in the palm of Daniella's hand. She closed her hand tightly around him.

"Regardless of your circumstance, you will focus on the sound of my voice," she said. "You will pay attention to me, not the discomfort you feel," she said as she gripped him firmly, pressing his balls between her fingertips and the heel of her palm. "Do you understand?"

"Yes, Master," he replied, trying to keep his voice steady.

* * *

When Daniella had initially taken Tom as a servant to her in her home, they established a division of domestic chores. She sat on the sofa in the living room and had him kneel before her. She had a pad of paper on which she took notes, creating a document for him to memorize. As it was for many young women, this was an enjoyable exercise. She began listing all of the household chores she would assign to her new husband.

"I feel like just writing the word *everything,* but that wouldn't be all that helpful to you, would it?" she joked. "Instead, we will begin by assigning you all outdoor maintenance and yard work," she said as she began writing her list for him. "That means mow the lawn, obviously, and trim the hedges and whatnot. Keep the lawn as perfectly manicured and flawless as you keep your body," she said with a wink. "It's what everyone will see when they come to the house. I mean the lawn, not your body," she said with a laugh. "Though who knows? Some of my friends will be allowed to see you naked, maybe some others as well. We will see."

She stroked the side of his face in an affectionate way.

"Anyway, you'll be assigned the interior of the home as well," she said. "That includes the bathrooms, first and foremost. I want them impeccably, exquisitely clean. The counters, sinks, bathtubs, and showers, but most importantly, the toilets will be spectacularly clean. Even the mirrors will be spotless. In the kitchen, I'll want the floor, counters, and all other surfaces to be clean, neat, and well-organized. The entirety of the rest of the house will be clean. Rugs and carpets will be vacuumed, and hardwood floors will be swept and polished. You will wash and dry, the laundry and place clean clothes in the drawers and closets, everything where it belongs. Where I will expect it to be. You will complete all of your chores before I come home in the evening, when I may have other demands of you. Do you understand your obligations as I've assigned them?"

"Yes, Master," he replied. "Thank you for your instruction."

"Good," she said with a smile. "Now get to work."

Tom began with cleaning each of the bathrooms, but after Daniella inspected his work, she called him to the living room.

"The downstairs bathroom is not as clean as I would like it to be," she said. "What punishment would be most effective in encouraging you to work harder to exceed my expectations?"

His body noticeably lowered in height and seemed to shrink somewhat in size. He had an expression of disappointment on his face.

"I apologize, Master," he said. "If it pleases you, several multiples of ten with the ruler would be a corrective encouragement for me."

"That does please me, though I regret the reason for its necessity," she said. "I'm annoyed that I have to reprimand you, Tom. I have enough to do without being in charge of supervising your assigned tasks. Fetch the ruler."

Tom quickly retrieved the wooden ruler, a solid piece of hardwood she employed in situations where he forgot his place. Originally, the implement had looked to him as though it would be far less effective than it would turn out to be. It left a sharp, stinging welt when she used it to spank his bare butt.

"Present," she said, pointing to the floor.

She used the word *present* as a shortened form of the phrase *present yourself for punishment*. She employed the word often in speaking to Tom.

"I will do you the favor of reminding you that if your body should move in any direction while I apply each set of ten strokes of the ruler, then they will not count toward your total, and I will have to start over from the beginning."

"Yes, Master," he replied. "Thank you, Master."

"It is so important to me that you try harder," she said. "I want to see you working toward a more rewarding life for both of us. I can see a future for us where all of my needs and wants are met and exceeded and you are constantly achieving the goals I've set for you in your submission and obedience to me. You want that too, right?"

"Yes, absolutely," he replied. "Thank you, Master."

"I'm doing you a favor in allowing you to receive correction for your mistake," she said. "You will best be deeply grateful for the privilege of enduring my punishment. Because it won't happen often, if at all, that I will allow a boy to endure excruciating pain in exchange for forgiveness. So I want you to be very present in the moment and feel every sensation while I punish you. If it hurts, I want to know. So don't be shy. Just give me what I want."

She began paddling his ass with the wooden ruler at a slow and steady pace, taking her time in laying each crimson stripe across his bare ass.

"That's so cute," she said. "I can really see how painful this is for you."

Once she'd delivered around fifty sharply stinging strokes with the ruler, turning his butt a blushing dark pink, she ordered him to fetch the largest of her collection of butt plugs. He lubricated it, then brought it to her and assumed the position. She pressed the tip of the plug against his asshole.

"Do you understand why you needed to be punished and fitted with this butt plug?" she asked.

"Yes, Master," he replied.

"And do you see how I have followed the only correct course of action in response?" she asked.

"Yes, Master," he replied. "And thank you, Master."

She pressed firmly, driving the plug deep into his asshole. He managed to keep from crying out while keeping his body relaxed.

"You will have your ass plugged until I say different," she said.

"May I go attempt to correct my mistake in failing to exceed your expectations in cleaning the bathroom, or do you need anything right now?" he asked.

She thought for a moment.

"No, you're free to get to work," she said.

"Thank you, Master," he replied.

* * *

As she usually preferred to do upon coming home after work, Daniella was lying on the sofa, while Tom knelt on the floor before her and massaged her feet.

"So, you remember my mentioning the boy I apprehended earlier in the week, the one I told you about?" she asked. "He's your boss's ex-husband?"

"Yes, you mentioned arresting him," Tom replied. "His name is Charlie, I believe?"

"Yeah, him," Daniella said. "Does she ever talk about him?"

"Not really," Tom replied. "She doesn't talk with me about things like that, and it isn't really common knowledge, either."

"Yes, right there," Daniella sighed, indicating the part of her foot he was massaging. "Fuck, you're talented. Anyway, yeah, I can imagine that no one would want to spend their time talking about that asshole. By the way, do the women you work with pinch your butt?"

Tom laughed.

"No, of course not," he replied. Why do you ask?"

"I don't know, you've got such a cute butt," she said. "I would, if I worked there."

"I believe it is out of respect for you that they refrain from doing so," Tom replied. "Otherwise, perhaps they would."

"Hmm. Well, so this boy we detained, your boss's ex-whatever, I gave him a pretty good beating today," she said. "A bit of a lecture as well. I could see that he would have had a fully erect penis if not for the chastity device. Like all boys, once you show them what their submission should look like, their body responds. What a fucking idiot. Anyway, it's put me in a mood. I'm going to want your tongue worshipping me."

"Yes, Master," Tom replied, his desire quite evident in his voice.

"You want that?" she asked in a teasing voice. "You want to give me a ride on your expertly trained tongue?"

"Yes, Master," Tom replied. "I want that desperately."

"Desperately?" she asked. I like the sound of that. Crawl for me," she commanded him.

Daniella relocated to the bedroom, where she undressed, and climbed onto the bed. She was lying on her back, her bronze skin in contrast to the white bedsheets, with her long, shapely legs spread wide and her knees bent slightly and her back arched in anticipation. She had one hand behind her head on the pillow while the other hand absent-mindlessly caressed and pinched her nipples.

Tom entered the bedroom, crawling on his hands and knees, and positioned himself between her thighs with his tongue attending to her pleasure in the way she'd trained him to. He held her by the hips, which he knew from experience would start to buck when he brought her close to orgasm. He knew to keep his tongue is service of her clit regardless. His mind was focused completely on her body and its desire.

Tom had been in this precise position countless times, for up to an hour at a time as often as once and occasionally twice a day. The taste and the scent of Daniella's pussy was so much a part of his life that it felt like it was the most constant part of his concept of home. Her body was so elemental to his idea of being at home that he felt he was an extension of her. It was as though he was as an appendage of her body that she could reattach at any time, his mouth being the part that aligned with her pussy in the attachment. She thought of his body in much the same way.

"By the way, my boyfriend is coming over tomorrow night," Daniella said while Tom was worshipping her pussy.

Tom was unsure of which boyfriend she was talking about. He wondered if it was Darius, who was remarkably well-hung.

"Oh, and we're going over to visit with Sonia tomorrow," she said. "I mean your boss. Your boss lady." Daniella affectionately combed her fingers through Tom's hair. "Well, I'm your boss lady. I mean your *other* boss lady."

Tom slid his tongue upward, keeping it flat as he lapped up the wetness that dripped from her pussy, then gradually drew it into a point as he slipped it between her labia and curled upward to caress her clit. He drew his tongue into his mouth and swallowed, tasting her, then repeated the motion. She liked it when he wasn't in any hurry and took his time in warming up her body before he began worshipping her pussy with the devotion he invariably displayed for her.

"That's perfect, Tom," she sighed.

Tom felt a surge of pleasure that was greater than any other he could imagine when he heard the sound of Daniella's contentment. He felt himself sinking deep into the depths of her sexual ecstasy, a warm, beautiful place that enveloped him like a fog. A place where his only thoughts were of her—her scent, her taste, and most importantly, her intimately unique expression of female desire. He forgot himself momentarily and surrendered to worshipping her body and her mind, paying tribute to her as his owner and his commander, but also as master of his body, mind, and spirit.

Chapter 11

"Officer Fuerza," Sonia Taylor said warmly as Daniella and Tom were escorted by Ms. Taylor's butler into a room in the back of the house where Sonia preferred to receive guests. "Please, have a seat," she said, indicating a couch opposite the armchair in which Sonia was seated.

Sonia was intrigued by the policewoman, who was wearing a long, sleeveless dress that revealed her impressive muscularity beneath its soft, draping fabric.

"Thank you for having us over, Ms. Taylor," Daniella replied as she took a seat. She made a pointing gesture, to which Tom responded by kneeling beside her on the floor.

Sonia smiled approvingly at Tom's effortless obedience.

"Harry, bring us each something to drink," Sonia said to her butler. "I've been so enamored with this peach cocktail as of late. Might you like one?" she asked Daniella.

"I'm not on duty, so yes, please," she replied. "Tom would like a glass of water."

"Of course," she said with a nod toward Harry. "Now, I suggest we do away with formalities. You may call me Sonia if you will permit me to call you Daniella?"

"Yes, of course," Daniella replied. "Thank you, Sonia."

"We haven't met but I feel that I know a little about you simply because I've seen the result of your influence on Tom," Sonia said. "So, I've been looking forward to meeting the woman into whose account Tom's paycheck is deposited," Sonia said. "And by the way, it would be more, but we've recently hired a young woman as an assistant intern, and as you know, I can't very well pay him more than her."

"I understand, you have a legal obligation in that regard," Daniella said.

"But I feel you should feel proud of your accomplishments in his training," Sonia said. "He is a well-trained boy, and I'm sure that it has much to do with your having put some effort into his conditioning."

"Thank you," Daniella replied. "I'm not shy in applying the whip."

"All of the women I work with have discussed his obedience, and I've yet to hear anyone claiming that his behavior is wanting of any corrective measure," Sonia said. "I wonder how you've been so effective. As you know, I myself have failed in that regard. My ex-husband has, unfortunately, fallen into your capable hands for guidance and correction."

"You've been very successful in so many of your ventures," Daniella said, "I'm not sure that its fair to blame yourself for Charlie's failings. I know that when I met Tom, he was already very aware of his place in relation to me. He required little effort, really. I think that some boys just take more work to get them into a proper alignment."

"I regret not being more demanding of Charlie," Ms. Taylor said. "I think I was focused on my company and my career and perhaps I should have focused more on training him. More focused on denial and command."

"Well, he's getting a lot of that right now," Daniella said with a bright smile. "But it shouldn't be a woman's responsibility to make a boy compliant. They should take that on themselves. You've every right to have focused your attention on building the life you wanted for yourself."

"I suppose you're right. But I think that perhaps the problem was that at first, I was hesitant to punish him," Sonia admitted. "I kept thinking of the way that I would feel in his situation. Eventually I came to understand that it's one of those differences in gender. At first, I hadn't really grasped how the male body and mind are uniquely formed to not only respond to, but essentially thrive when given discipline. I have come to learn that it was a biological response unique to the male body."

"I've found that to be true," Daniella said.

Harry reentered the room with a tray, offering the drinks he'd prepared to Daniella and Sonia, and allowing Tom to take his glass of water.

"What a woman might think of as torture is actually cathartic and freeing to the male mind and body," Daniella said. "But it should feel natural. Each woman should find a method of punishment that works for her. It should be something that feels comfortable for her to employ and effective for the male. At least, that's been my experience."

"I'm sure that you know what you are talking about," Sonia said. "It's good that there are women like yourself providing such a valuable public service. I've seen how, left to their own devices, boys will often make poor decisions," Sonia said with a sigh.

"A method I employ with Tom involves penetrating his ass with a butt plug before I assign him his tasks," Daniella said. "Not a small one. Enormous, rather. Then I'll send him off to do his domestic chores."

"I'm sure that's effective," Sonia said. "You know, there used to be a stigma about anal penetration of the male body. They were so hesitant to talk about or admit how much they loved it. Many of them were even convinced that they didn't want it, in spite of the biological fact that it was incredibly stimulating to the male body. It was just a social construct, really, a collective fear they had, which we would eventually overcome. Then, when it was not only safe for a boy to admit his desire, but it also became advantageous for a boy to openly express his ability to accept penetration of remarkable size. Bragging, really, showing his obedience by taking it in the ass, the bigger and harder, the better."

Daniella laughed.

"It helps to ensure that he remains focused on the goals set for him," Daniella said. "And it is the female's responsibility to see that he accepts his subordinate role in their relationship. As I'm sure you know, the mind of those of the male gender is not suited to seeing the big picture in the way that the female mind does. They have their charms, for sure, but making decisions about large-scale, comprehensive issues is not their strong suit. They are best relegated to making choices from a preselected set of options. They thrive in an environment we establish for them. They will come to appreciate our guidance once we've clearly defined the boundaries. Much like any other element of your life, the male servant needs to be conditioned to respond to the protocols you set for them."

"I guess that it's one of those things that I'm well-aware of, but in actual practice, I tend to falter in being consistent," Sonia admitted. "I mean, I know that it is the woman's right, and more importantly her responsibility, to create a structured, well-defined environment for her male. One where he understands her expectations of him, and his schedule and how he spends his time are decided for him. But again, I believe that I didn't pay attention to this dynamic in the way that I should have."

"Yeah, well, perhaps it is for the best," Daniella replied. "I'm sure that you've no trouble in acquiring boys with which to amuse yourself?"

Sonia laughed.

"No, I suppose not," she replied. "In fact, I've recently gotten my hands on this beautiful boy, scandalously young, and deeply responsive to my command. But again, I tend to indulge myself in ways that may be counter to my own interests. As we know, one of the important elements of practicing control of the male body is orgasm denial."

"Right," Daniella replied. She glanced at Tom, who nodded in agreement. "Is it good for the female body and mind to be denied orgasm? Absolutely not. Is it good for the male body and mind to be denied orgasm? Unequivocally, yes. In all of the research that I've read, It's been made clear that orgasm denial is one of the best things we can do in promoting healthy male minds and bodies. I mean, if I hear a woman say that her slave-husband is unlocked once a year, and he looks proud to have her say as much about him, it means that he has sublimated his own desires in deference to her. And that has been a consistent part of our relationship," Daniella said, then glanced at Tom. "Tom is not allowed to orgasm with anything approaching regularity."

"Perhaps it's a weakness on my part," Sonia confessed, "that I've always loved making boys come. I love watching him make a mess all over himself. It's partly why I love younger males, they tend to, you know. Ejaculate. A lot. It's incredible, really."

"Well, there's no reason why you shouldn't do whatever you like," Daniella said. "I do make my boyfriends come, just not my husband."

"So, you have boyfriends?" Sonia asked. "I take it they're just playthings for you?"

"Yes, exactly," Daniella replied. "I've enough responsibility just owning the one husband," she said, patting Tom on the head in an affectionate way.

"I understand that," Sonia said, "but I can say that I work with a number of women who've found that though one husband might seem like a lot of responsibility, two or more were, paradoxically, less so. They generally find that the presence of an additional male or more will actually help in guiding each of the individual males. It's just a suggestion. Perhaps you might think about it as an option."

"I have thought about it," Daniella replied. "For now, I just have my boyfriends for entertainment. Nothing serious."

"It's funny, but it used to be that the term *second husband* referred to a situation in which a woman had gotten divorced and remarried," Sonia said. "It was not common for a woman to have more than one husband back then."

"I've heard that divorce was more common as well," Daniella said.

"When the law was changed, and boys were no longer allowed to initiate a divorce, it happened less frequently," Sonia said. "My own unfortunate situation notwithstanding. But overall, women became empowered to change the situation to one where neither of the two in a partnership even wanted that. Modifying the rights available to boys took care of a variety of problems, it turned out."

"That comes up in my line of work quite frequently," Daniella said. "When we arrived at our current set of laws in which those of the male gender had little, if anything, in the way of rights, they came to appreciate their position in a more meaningful way."

"But they eventually saw it how it was to their benefit," Sonia said. "I mean, they do now. So tell me how the two of you met. I'm always fascinated by that aspect of any relationship."

"We met at a CFNM party," Daniella admitted, laughing.

"Oh, that's charming," Sonia replied. "I imagine then that the dynamic between the two of you was instituted immediately."

"Pretty much," Daniella said. She reached over and grabbed a handful of hair on the back of Tom's head and pulled his head back in an aggressive manner. "He did need a bit of conditioning and training, but like I said, he was pretty well-adjusted when we met."

"You know," Sonia said, "that takes me back a bit to when it was new. The social restructuring, I mean. We'd have these parties where we'd strip the boys naked. It was an exhilarating time and women were getting comfortable with their authority. And boys too, I guess, they were getting comfortable with their submission. So we'd have all the boys take off their clothes for us, just to do it, really. Just because we could. It was like this celebration, really. We could tell the boys they'd be naked, and they'd just follow orders. There was a novelty to it. Oh, and the women could get so ornery, making the boys do all manner of things. It was so much fun when that was happening."

"I can imagine," Daniella replied, smiling at the thought.

Sonia smiled wistfully and paused for a moment.

"There was this one party," Sonia said, "and I had just taken this new job. Basically, it was the job my boss had previously held. He was now under my authority. And so when I walked into this party, there was my old boss who was now a member of my staff. What surprised me was that he looked so good naked, better than I would have imagined. I walked up to him and said hello, and he turned bright red from embarrassment.," she said, laughing at the memory. "It was delicious, this reversal. He had not been the easiest person to work for. So, I decided to get a little bit of revenge. I actually thought it would be good for him to be put in his place and definitely cathartic for me. I humiliated the fuck out of him," she said, laughing. "I got ahold of a length of rope," she explained. "I tied it around his balls, and the other ends went around each ankle. I made it short, so that he could not quite stand up and had to waddle around, hearing all of the women laugh at his predicament.

Daniella laughed at the image in her mind, but she also cataloged the method of bondage for her own use with Tom.

"I will admit that it was kind of fun back then," Sonia said. "It felt dangerous in a way. There were these boys who felt they had to be secretive about their desires, and they were terrified of being outed. They would only admit to a compulsion to submit to female authority in private. Now, that's not to say that it was better. It wasn't, not compared to now, having all of society correctly oriented. But again, there was something exciting about doing it in private, especially with boys who thought it was something dirty and shameful. I know that sounds weird saying it now. There is nothing dirty or shameful about female domination, rather, it's the most natural state of being. But it had this glorious effect on boys. They'd be so embarrassed by my putting them in their place, and it made them blush and look so cute. They knew how much control they were handing over. It was touching, really, to see these brave, naked boys trembling with fear, but still, they'd kneel and obey. My female friends and I would speak openly to one another about the ones who had already evolved to submit. It was exciting, really. We had no idea what was coming, or how quickly it would happen. It was so exciting watching the world just turn like that."

"I imagine," Daniella said, "but I'm happy to be on the other side of it."

"Oh, I've forgotten to mention that I saw your video yesterday," Sonia said. "It was so deeply satisfying for me to watch Charlie get what he deserves. Thank you for that."

"You are more than welcome," Daniella said, "but really, I'm just doing my job. Oh, and I wanted to ask you something. Charlie will likely be given corporal punishment when we bring him before the judge. It will be significantly harsher than what I delivered the other day, and more public. In addition, he'll be given a hefty fine, as well as community service under the direction of a female guardian assigned by the judge. If you have any interest in being the woman charged with supervising his service, I could make that recommendation to the judge. Most likely he'll be required to report to you for assignment until he has completed one hundred hours of service, though it could be more."

"I would have to think about that," Sonia said. "It's a question of time. I'd be happy to have him working his little butt off, but the supervision would require my input, I suppose."

"Right, he would need your signature on his progress," Daniella said. "If at any time he fails to get a signature for successful completion of each assignment of his service, he would have to report back to the court for an additional judgment. This would mean additional punishment, an additional fine, and an extension of his service requirement."

"I wonder if I could effectively outsource his supervision," Sonia wondered aloud. "I could have my boy Aaron providing oversight."

"That would be entirely acceptable to the court, as far as I know," Daniella replied. "As long as you were happy with the arrangement."

"Well, that sounds like a plan," Sonia said, laughing at the thought.

"Speaking of plans, we should probably get going," Daniella said.

"Of course," Sonia said. "It was lovely to meet you, Daniella, and I look forward to having you over again sometime soon."

"Likewise, Sonia, and I look forward to seeing you soon as well," Daniella replied.

Chapter 12

"Sonia is impressive," Daniella said as she started up the car and put it in drive. "You have an impressive boss lady," she added, giving him a gentle squeeze on his thigh.

"Well, like you said, she's my *other* boss lady," he replied. "And yes, I have two impressive boss ladies."

"You know, I made such an excellent choice the evening we met," Daniella said. "When Sonia asked about it, it kind of took me back to our first conversation. I loved how nervous you were," she said with a smile. She slid her hand up his thigh. Her little finger could feel his chastity cage brushing against it. "And to think that you weren't even locked at that point."

"You took care of that fairly soon after," Tom said. "For which I am eternally grateful."

"You're so welcome," Daniella replied as she stroked his locking device but kept her eyes on the road. "But the thing that was so funny about it was that you showed up to the party with no idea it was naked males only. I so loved that."

"Not the most intimidated I've felt around you, but right up there," Tom replied.

* * *

The colored lights strung all around the backyard reflected off the surface of the pool. As Daniella sat observing the party guests mingling, talking, drinking, and laughing, she amused herself with the sight of the various men, stripped and exposed, each presented for her to examine. As she slowly perused the sight before her, she stopped and focused on one specific element: a gorgeously well-built man standing alone, looking more vulnerable than any she'd seen in quite some time. He brought to mind the boys she first had cornered while playing outside in her neighborhood while growing up. He had that naïve and innocent quality she'd seen when she'd first ordered boys to strip naked for her to examine. The way they'd tremble, intimidated by her personal influence and power.

She stood and crossed the patio to confront him.

"Tell me how it felt when you learned you had to strip naked," Daniella asked Tom, obviously enjoying the predicament he'd found himself in.

"Well, I guess I was kind of terrified, to tell the truth," he replied.

"Ooh, that's a nice start," she said. "I love it when you boys get scared. But then what? Did you kind of have to wrestle with it in your mind? Like, decide if you were brave enough to be completely exposed to all the women here?"

"Yeah, it was kind of like that," he admitted.

She was enjoying herself, he realized, and there was something Tom found disarmingly attractive about seeing her take pleasure in his feeling discomfort.

"I was afraid that it would be sort of humiliating to have to be completely naked," he admitted.

"Sort of?" she asked. "How about *totally* humiliating? Come on, admit it."

"OK, yes. Totally humiliating," he admitted.

"Ha-ha!" she exclaimed. "That's exactly why I came here tonight. I wanted to see some men stripped naked and completely humiliated. Like you," she added, glancing up and down his body. "You have a small penis," she said, flashing a brilliant smile. "I like that."

"Um, what?" he responded. "I'm sorry, that's just, uh, I didn't expect that," he stammered.

"Really?" she asked. "I'd think you'd have gotten used to it," she said, examining his endowment.

"I'm generally not naked when I meet someone," he said. "So, they don't notice my, um . . . ."

"Tiny penis?" she asked.

"Right," he replied.

"Say it," she said.

"They don't see my tiny penis," he said.

"Good boy," she said. "So, right, then obviously, you complied," she said. "You took off your clothes and you walked out here. Have the women here tonight made you feel objectified, maybe? Has it been as embarrassing to you personally as you feared it might be?"

"To be truthful, yes, but I'm adjusting to it, I think," he said.

"And what does a boy like you do for work?" she asked.

"I'm an executive assistant," he replied.

"So, you serve at the pleasure of a female superior?" she teased.

"Literally that," he replied.

"Well, that's kind of impressive as well," she said. "I imagine you've got to be really responsive to female authority to keep that job."

"As the only male in the executive department, they absolutely keep me on my toes," he replied.

"I like that visual," she said.

"May I ask you the same question?" he asked.

"You may," she replied. "I'm a cop."

"So, you're law enforcement?" he asked. "That's impressive. And intimidating."

"It's the handcuffs, isn't it?" she said with a brilliant smile.

"Partly," he said. He tried not to stare at her powerfully shaped body. Tom felt his attraction to her increasing exponentially. Her physicality was such that he thought of a powerful creature from the wild, something predatory and untamed, or perhaps a machine whose exquisitely built, advanced technology made her body a lethal and formidable weapon. All of this gave perspective on her enigmatic gaze, which was simultaneously alluring and terrifying.

"The thing is, Tom, when I meet a boy who captures my interest, I have him," Daniella explained. "As in, I take him and do as I please. Without limitation. It's just the way it is, since that is the way I am. Thing is, Tom, I'm somewhat interested in you. I'm curious to see if you are capable of being the kind of infinitely submissive boy I require."

"Infinitely submissive?" Tom asked.

"Yes," she replied. "You're unfamiliar with the concept?"

"I apologize, it's just that—" he began.

"I'm not interested in your apology, Tom," she interrupted. "Just your obedience. There are rules," she explained. "Show me that you can follow the rules and I will reward you. Disobey and I will punish you. Do you want me to punish you?"

"No, Master," he replied.

"Good," she concluded. "Now, do understand that I do not refer to certain things as punishment, things that you may think of that way. For instance, I enjoy inflicting pain on the male body. This is not punishment. It's fun. I like it. I will whip your naked body with a number of implements, frequently, but it is not necessarily to punish you. Believe me, you will know when I am beating your cute little ass for punishment. Other times, it'll just be for my pleasure. Understand?"

"But I—" he began.

"Woah, hold up," she interrupted him. "That's where you say 'Yes, Master.' I am not interested in whatever you think about what I've communicated to you. I want your compliance, not your input."

"Yes, Master," he replied softly.

"Louder," she said.

"Yes, Master," he repeated.

"Show me your balls," she demanded.

"I'm um," Tom replied, looking down at his naked body and thinking she could see them already. He realized that she meant *display* them to her. He lifted his balls in his hand, holding them up for her to examine. She looked him in the eye for some moments, then lowered her gaze.

"They're actually a nice size," she commented.

Tom lowered them and removed his hand.

"Stop," she commanded. "Hold them up and show me your balls like I told you to. I'll tell you when you can stop."

Tom paused, but then complied with the order.

"Ah, good boy," Daniella said. "I like obedience, by the way. If you couldn't tell, I'm completely dominant."

"I gathered that," Tom said with a smile.

"Well, now that you have your balls displayed for me, appropriately, I'm going to tell you a few things," she said. "As I mentioned, I am a supremely dominant female. And I tend to rate boys by the quality of their submission to me," she said. "It is the appearance of effortlessness that I am looking for. I want to see that it feels natural for the boy in question to submit."

"Am I the boy in question?" he asked.

"At the moment, yes," she said. She observed him closely. "I am contemplating what use you might be to me."

He tried to remain still while displaying his balls in his hand.

"Like any female, I am comfortable in a position of authority in regard to someone of your gender," she said, "but I am also fiercely and unapologetically dominant. I am a sadist as well. The boys who serve me are required to submit to physical punishment in submission to me. When I consider a male for use in entertaining myself, I pay particular attention to his capability in enduring punishment. You boys are so attractive when you're writhing in pain. Your naked bodies are so delicious in their vulnerability and subjugation. And I have an appreciation for hard, submissive cock," she said.

She gave him a wink.

"Hey," she said to a woman who was walking past at that moment. "Take a look at this boy. What are the rules concerning boys getting an erection without permission?"

The woman examined Tom.

"There isn't any rule, per se," she said. "But I think you can do whatever you want, right? They aren't going to dare disobey when we've got them naked."

"I absolutely agree with that," Daniella replied, laughing.

"Yeah, we're pretty much free to subjugate them," the woman said. "Naked submission is expected, even."

"That's what I thought should be the case," Daniella replied. She turned her attention back to Tom.

"Hands up, behind your head," she commanded.

Tom complied, assuming the position. It crossed his mind that she was a cop as she stepped up beside him and placed her hand on his butt cheek. She gave it a squeeze.

"Oh, that's nice," Daniella said. "I bet you look so cute when you've been spanked, with a nice rosy glow to your cheeks," she observed. "I do believe you might be the type of boy I am looking for to serve me as a slave," she said, smiling warmly as she continued stroking his bare ass with her fingertips.

They had been dating just over two months when she decided to keep Tom locked in chastity on a permanent basis.

"I don't like it when you come," Daniella said. "It makes you lazy and arrogant. I want you to be on edge, so you respond quicker when I snap my fingers. You'll be locked up nice and secure, and you won't be having any orgasms unless I specifically allow them. Which I will not."

It was just after a year before Daniella proposed that Tom would assume the role of slave-husband.

Tom signed the documents giving her power of attorney and place all of his assets in Daniella's name. He gave up all legal claims in making decisions and had his paychecks deposited directly into her bank account.

He understood that legally, he was her property, and that he was expected to be obedient to her at all times. He endeavored to follow her orders without hesitation and put her needs before his own. For Tom, it was a far better existence committing himself to Daniella's servitude than anything he'd experienced previously.

* * *

When Daniella and Tom arrived home, she had just enough time for a luxuriously relaxing bath before her boyfriend Darius was scheduled to arrive.

"OK, naked, now," she said to Tom. "Run me a bath, do a once-over on the house to check that it's in order, and make sure the bedroom is ready."

"Yes, Master," Tom replied, already half undressed.

The bedroom she'd mentioned was not their main bedroom, but what she occasionally referred to as the guest bedroom. The guests were any of the boyfriends she'd have over on occasion, generally males who were remarkably well-endowed.

"I'll explain it to you," Daniella had said early in their relationship, before she'd even considered the idea of having Tom as a husband. "I was attracted to you immediately, and that most definitely included your tiny penis. I wanted a boy who is docile, obedient, and all that. Your cute little penis makes you super-submissive. I mean, what choice do you have, really? But then I also want a big, fat cock. But seriously, all the time? Absolutely not. Sometimes, yeah. But I'll actually end up feeling sore afterward. I want it, I get off on it, but then I'm satisfied, and I want to put it back in the drawer for next time. So I'll have occasional boyfriends, boys who know that they have a really specific use. I don't love them. I love you."

She kissed him, and Tom felt a sensation he'd never felt before. It was something he could only compare to having been in a jacuzzi outside while it was snowing while visiting friends in their winter cabin. Or having dived into a pool of ice water snowmelt while hiking on a blistering hot day. It was a contradiction, two conflicting feelings, both of which caused him excitation to an extreme.

"I love you too, Master," he'd said in return.

Tom attended to running a bath for Daniella, then lit what she referred to as the "unreasonable number of candles" placed throughout the bathroom. Then he stripped the bed in the guest bedroom to its white cotton sheet and lit a similar number of candles throughout the room. He went downstairs and began going through a mental checklist to see that everything was to Daniella's specifications.

When the doorbell rang, he answered it, unbothered by his being naked aside from his chastity lock.

"You should strip down and unlock yourself," Tom said to Darius, who was a few minutes early. "She's still getting ready, but she's in one of those moods, you know?"

"Yeah, I'm familiar," Darius replied. "Thank you for the heads up."

Tom was about to turn back to finishing his task when Darius got his attention.

"Have I told you you're the luckiest motherfucker?" Darius asked, a look of sincerity on his handsome, masculine face.

"You have," Tom replied. "And yeah, thank you. I am."

"Seriously, I try not to feel jealous," he said, "and remind myself to be respectful and grateful. But to be her slave? Her property? I can only imagine."

"We each have our place, I guess," Tom said. "Each of us doing our part in service. You know. Just doing whatever she wants. What she deserves."

When Daniella was done with her bath, she dried off and applied lotion to the entirety of her body. She preferred to remain fully nude when she had her boyfriends over, enjoying the commanding presence her magnificently powerful, muscular naked body projected. She entered the bedroom to find Darius as she preferred him to be, which was sitting on the end of the bed. She liked pushing him down and straddling his body, then reversing herself to face Tom, who was positioned on his knees at the foot of the bed.

Daniella straddled Darius, then took ahold of his massive dick. She positioned it so that the tip of his cock was aligned perfectly between her labia. Then she lowered herself onto his shaft, slowly, gradually taking the entirety of his length.

"Yeah, that's right," she said directly to Tom. "It feels even bigger than it looks."

As she took his length inside of her, she emitted a soft moan of ecstasy as she bottomed out, feeling the length and girth of his massive cock filling her pussy.

She reached out and brought Tom's face up against her body.

"Lick me," she commanded, directing Tom to pleasure her, following her movement up and down and keeping his tongue on her clit. She kept one hand on the back of his head while she fucked Darius with a slow, grinding rhythm.

Tom knew, because Daniella had explained to him that it was his tongue that made her orgasm.

"Having my boyfriend's big fucking rod in my pussy is hot, and I love it, but it's your tongue on my clit that actually puts me over the edge," she'd said.

Tom and Darius both knew exactly when Daniella would come, since she was the least self-conscious woman either of them had met when it came to how loudly she exclaimed her feelings of ecstasy. She was not shy about the neighbors hearing as well, as she did not restrain herself in her pursuit of pleasure in any way.

When Daniella's orgasm had subsided, she lifted herself off of Darius's cock, and sat on his lower abdomen, positioning herself such that when she began stroking his slick, hard shaft, it looked like it was attached to her own body. She leaned back and focused on Tom.

"Make him come, honey," she said as she took Tom by the back of his head and brought his mouth to Darius's engorged cockhead and pushed his head down on his massive shaft. She leaned back and watched, her hand remaining on the back of Tom's head.

"Suck it hard," she encouraged him. "Take it deep, show me how much you want to drain his cock for me."

Daniella began to play with her clit, bringing herself to another orgasm while she watched her boyfriend come, unloading into her husband's mouth.

"That's right, swallow every drop for me," Daniella said.

Chapter 13

Charlie sat on the cot in his cell and tried to sort through his wildly conflicting thoughts. The ideas he'd been confronted with remained swirling about within his head. Lectures, monologues, videos he'd been made to watch, Daniella and the other officers, each voice echoing in his brain.

"You want to accept it, you truly do, because you know that it is right," Charlie had heard repeatedly. "Down deep inside, you've always really known it. Haven't you?"

Did he? Charlie wondered. What was it he'd actually felt when confronted with the idea of being submissive to the female gender?

"You can admit it to me," he'd heard Officer Fuerza say into his ear. "I've been witness to many, many boys who've finally come to a place where they are able to surrender," she'd said. "It will be so deeply cathartic for you to do so. You simply state the truth. Your gender is not equal the female gender. You know it, and all you need to do is confess. Confess that you know it to be true. That you've always known it. Somewhere inside of you, a voice in the back of your head. Submission to female authority."

Impossibly, Charlie had felt his penis twitch in response. It had aroused him. Was it that the beautiful young woman who'd arrested him was personally so sexually desirable? Or was it the fact of her unquestioned authority over him that had so affected him?

"Perhaps it made your penis hard when the idea first crossed your mind," she'd said. "Or maybe it made you feel angry. Or sad. These are natural reactions. You were afraid that you would lose something that belonged to you."

Fear, Charlie thought. *Is that it? Am I afraid?*

He thought about the meditation exercises he'd been assigned, and the soundtrack to the videos he'd been given to watch:

"Imagine the loving embrace of a female superior, allowing you a place in service to her. You will finally be at peace, no longer wrestling with your bloated ego which has you denying what is staring you in the face. All you have to do is kneel, surrender, confess, and submit, acknowledging that we are undeniably and overwhelmingly more powerful than you are. Your place is at our feet, genuflecting in tribute to our natural supremacy. Know your place. Submit. Then, and only then will you be free. Free of the misguided notion that you are anything even approaching our equal. Commit yourself to service, and you will have a place in the world. Continue with your delusion of equality and you will have nothing."

Charlie couldn't help but feel the meditation working in causing him to become more relaxed. Was its message getting through to him as well? Or the lecture by a woman named Emma Halston, who'd been introduced as professor of Gynarchic Studies, in which she'd explained that "Political, social, and interpersonal power is of two distinct types. That which women wield is a total, comprehensive power. It is far-reaching, complete, and unquestionably superior to that which the male is allowed. For the male is, in fact, allowed, or given, a particular type of power. And that is the power of obedience and service to female rule."

Ms. Halston looked every bit the academic with her hair pulled back tightly as she lectured Charlie, who was positioned kneeling on the floor, naked and handcuffed.

"The male gender is gifted with the opportunity to serve its superiors by one, genuflecting at our feet. And two, offering itself to work in support of our goals, with the benefit of our guidance. The male gender has enjoyed the privilege of being given very specific guidance in everything it does. Women are remarkably giving and supportive in this regard. We have been infinitely generous in allowing boys to receive our instruction without limitation. To make it simpler, the clever ones will do as they're told without hesitation. The dumb ones will get punished."

She fixed Charlie with a look that suggested she was contemplating which of the two he was.

"Society has evolved into a female-dominated structure, celebrating feminism, gynarchy, female authority, and female supremacy," she continued to explain. "Women are the dominant cultural force, while those of the male gender assume a second-class status and answer to women as their natural leaders. Qualities such as empathy and compassion make women better suited for positions of power. Boys need to recognize and accept their natural role because they do have a subservient role to play in society. They are expected to follow instructions, prioritizing the happiness and needs of the female above their own. The male's purpose self-worth is tied to his ability to fulfill this role. By embracing female supremacy, boys can find fulfillment in supporting and elevating women, allowing them to succeed in positions of power and leadership."

And Charlie found that the assigned reading materials to be persuasive once he allowed himself to consider their message. In a book he was given to read whose title was *The Natural Order: male submission to Gynarchy,* he read:

"We've redefined masculinity as a submissive desire to please the dominant female, rather than to assert dominance and control. To fully embrace your status as a male, you must confront your weaknesses and accept your relative inferiority. This means letting go of the male ego and recognizing that your purpose is to serve. By acknowledging your weaknesses and embracing female power, you may find fulfillment in supporting women and contributing to a female-run world.

Breaking down the male ego and replacing it with a more submissive and compliant mindset is paramount. This process will involve both physical and psychological transformation, as you learn to internalize your role as a subordinate to the female gender.

You, as a member of the male gender, will need to fully commit to this ideal by acknowledging your relative inferiority and expressing your devotion to serving female power. Through this you will find liberation and fulfillment. Embracing your role as a submissive will allow you to find purpose and contentment in service to the superior female."

In a book titled *Serving the Superior Sex,* he read:

"Female supremacy is about simply encouraging males to embrace their role in being supportive and subordinate. It is about championing female leadership, and encouraging men to find fulfillment by supporting, elevating, and empowering women. By embracing their submissive role, those of the male gender can find satisfaction in the support of the female gender.

Females perform better when it comes to things such as self-control, self-motivation, dependability, sociability, perceptions of self-worth, a sense of agency in regard to her life, and delayed gratification. The bottom line is the female is smarter than the male, and the wisest thing for the male to do is to listen and follow directions."

In a society where female supremacy is the law, the male has evolved to serve the needs of women. The male's compulsion to obey has been harnessed to maximize women's control over those of the male gender, and it has become a powerful tool for manipulating them. They are assigned service and submission, which afforded them a sense of purpose.

Women are not equal to men. They are superior in many important ways. Males and females are fundamentally, biologically different in ways that affect behavior. These differences favor women, not men. A woman's brain has more neurons in the corpus callosum, which allows for better coordination between the brain's hemispheres. Consequently, the female brain is more highly developed structurally and functionally, and it is capable of thinking more soundly and intuitively than the male brain. Women are more insightful, and this doesn't even begin to address their greater stamina and longevity."

In the book *The Biology of Female Supremacy,* he read:

"The template of all biology is the female gender. At conception and in the first few weeks of gestation, all embryos are female. The male is simply a copy of the female and is therefore inferior to the female. To create a male, the woman's body must recognize the inferior Y chromosome present within the male's sperm, which is simply a damaged and mutated X chromosome. This damaged chromosome ends the development of female characteristics and forces the formation of the inferior male gender characteristics, and the baby is consigned to the role nature designed for the male of the species in service to the female. Female superiority is a provable scientific fact, and one has simply to observe reality to arrive at this conclusion.

And while the female is superior, this does not mean that the male is without purpose. Males are, owing to their design, subservient to their female superiors. The male must recognize that his true place is, in a matter of speaking, beneath the feet of his female superior. He exists to support her. It requires courage for the male to submit to the pain, suffering, humiliation, and denial it requires. But once the male has been taught, trained, corrected, and reeducated, they will find and assume their place in a female-dominant social structure.

And in *Breaking Them In: The Domination of the Subgender,* he read:

"The surrender of the male gender to the reality of female superiority was a beautiful thing for all of humanity to witness. All that was required was for males to simply acknowledge that the female gender is superior to their own. This is the method by which we transferred power from those that should never have had it to those that were beyond deserving of such power. It made the world a far better place once a gender-appropriate alignment of authority and power was established, where the natural gifts of the female were recognized and celebrated. Recognizing the natural limitations of the male was paramount in the transition to their becoming useful members of a gynarchy world order."

Charlie wanted to deny the thoughts in his head. He felt an urge to fight this compulsion he had to give in and accept what he was hearing. He thought that reason might be enough to challenge the notion that he surrender, but reason itself was what seemed to be working against him. Logically, the ideas he was being coerced into accepting were beginning to make sense.

But there was something far more persuasive in play, and that was his own body's reaction to the words being spoken into his ear. It was as though he was slowly losing his grip on what he'd so assuredly thought was his reality. In its place, a new, beguiling, and irresistible concept of his place in the world was beginning to form. He had begun to see himself differently.

Thoughts of kneeling before a powerful feminine entity, surrendering to a mystical force of nature, which had been like shadow figures in the far reaches of his mind, were becoming like solid matter. No longer were these merely thoughts, they were now transforming into undeniably real and tangible truths. But what he had previously identified a kind of restraint, ideas about his rightful place as binding him and forcing him into submission, he now began to see as a release from bondage. The metal device that so completely locked his penis into compliance had begun to feel like an object that was liberating him. The powerful force of manipulation that had so taken hold of him when he wasn't in chastity was now imprisoned, freeing his mind to accept what he had previously discarded: That obedience to female rule did not deny him his identity. It formed his identity. It provided him with a new, and higher purpose.

Charlie knelt on the concrete floor of his cell. He lowered himself onto his hands and knees, then extended his hands out before him until his forehead was touching the floor. He placed his palms flat against the cool, hard surface. He felt the vulnerability inherent his body's position, with his balls and his asshole presented without protection, offering them further by placing his knees and his hips just so, genuflecting to a powerful entity beyond his comprehension.

What had previously felt impossible, this offering himself to something he didn't understand, was beginning to feel natural and right. He began to realize that he couldn't be expected to understand it. He was not equipped to understand it, and it wasn't his place to do so. His place was to present himself as he was, offering his mind and body for a purpose, to be made use of by those more qualified than himself. In this positioning of his physical body, he felt himself surrendering his previous notion of himself and accepting a far better interpretation of who and what he was. He saw that his obedience was not something he offered, it was a gift being offered to him. It was a privilege he had yet to earn to show obedience and follow the guidance of his superiors.

Unbeknownst to Charlie, Officer Fuerza was at that moment standing outside his cell, observing his posture. He was situated such that his asshole was offered up in submission for her to view. She smiled at the sight of his willing subjugation of his body.

"See, that wasn't so hard, now was it, Charlie?" she murmured to herself.

She entered his cell and sat on the cot beside him. She observed him for a moment longer, then ordered him up onto his knees.

"Do you agree with me now that you deserve to be very publicly humiliated as punishment for your actions, Charlie?" Daniella asked. "And don't answer immediately. I know that you know the correct answer, but I want you to think about it first before you give a response. I want you to have really thought about what you have done and what you truly deserve as a result. Because your punishment won't mean as much, and it won't be as effective unless you entirely understand the ways in which you have earned it."

Charlie lowered his head, feeling shame course through him as a result of his having done precisely what the officer said, which was to have earned his punishment. He felt her hand raise his chin up.

"Don't lower your face, feeling sorry for yourself," she said in admonishment. "Grow up, be mature, and accept what is coming to you. You've been beaten. You lost. Admit it, accept it, and take responsibility for your obligation to submit and surrender. Think about it as a step toward a better future, one in which you learn to be a productive member of society in service to the women whose leadership you'll enjoy as a gift freely given to you."

Charlie looked directly at Daniella.

"I admit to having acted shamefully," he said. "I would be grateful for an opportunity to pay for the decisions I have made in the past and make reparations for my errors in judgement."

Daniella was impressed.

"Well, then," she said, "I am proud of you. It will not be easy for you, but it will be worth it if it motivates you in the right direction."

"May I have a punishment appropriate my disobedience?" he asked.

"I am pleased that you've shown maturity in recognizing your need for punishment," she said. "And yes, Charlie. We will be happy to provide you with what I am sure will feel like a relief for you. It will be painful, for sure, but it will be freeing for you to release your feelings of shame and humiliation."

Chapter 14

Violet was lying on her bed in her dorm room, and she had placed her arms up over her head in a pose of luxurious relaxation. She looked downward, over her body, at Theo, who she'd instructed to stand naked at the foot of her bed. She was wearing a white T-shirt and was otherwise naked. Theo loved how freely she exposed her pussy to him, though he had to try not to stare at it out of respect for her. He looked to her expectantly.

"Dance for me," she said.

"What? Dance?" he asked.

"Yes, Theo. Now," she said.

"There's no music," he protested.

"You want the belt?" she asked.

Theo started dancing, moving his hips around and stepping back and forth.

"No, come on, get into it," Violet said. "I want to see *good* dancing."

Theo took a breath, then put his hands up in the air and began moving his body in a sensual, serpentine motion.

"Yay!" Violet exclaimed, clapping her hands. "Keep going. Make it sluttier."

He slowly rotated and presented his ass in an overtly sexualized manner. He reached back and gave himself a spank on his butt cheek.

Violet whistled and laughed.

"Very cute," she said. "Now come here."

He crawled onto the bed to join her, lying beside her body on the bed. She kissed him, and then touched her fingertip to the tip of his nose.

"You're such a fun pet to play with, Theo," she said. "Say, what do you think about coming home with me this coming weekend. You can meet my family, and I want you to meet this woman, she's a neighbor of mine. She's been a really important influence in my life."

"I'd would be honored to," Theo replied. "I mean that, it's kind of a privilege to be introduced like that."

"How do you mean?" Violet asked.

"Just that when a woman decides that a boy has proven himself worthy of being introduced to the people in her life, that means something. I mean, if you want it to mean something."

Violet smiled, then kissed him.

"You like being submissive, right?" she asked. "You wouldn't want to be anything other than what you are? You know, I mean second-class status. Obedient to the female gender."

"I can't imagine anything else," he replied. He felt nothing but adoration of her, and wondered why she was asking him such a question.

"It's just that, I love the way you boys embrace your status as secondary to my gender," she said. "Like you just know that you belong to the servant class. I could never do that. I can't imagine having to submit."

"It's easy to accept when you're a boy," he said. "Women like yourself are so clearly deserving of your position.

"You know, when I was young, it never would have occurred to me to think that females were anything less than the dominant gender, or that boys were anything more than a servant class," Violet said. "It's just seemed natural that way."

"Of course," Theo said. "That's just how it is."

"I just want to know if you not just know your place, but truly love it," she said. "I could never be subjugated and made to submit the way it's expected of boys. I always think it would be humiliating for you to be made to kneel and serve and follow commands."

"I don't really think of it that way," he said. "Serving you is an honor for me."

"Yes, I guess it is," she said, smiling warmly. "And it's nice to watch you sink deeper into submission to me. I don't know why I said nice, that's such a tepid, kind of useless word. It's fantastic, or something like that. Gorgeous, beautiful. Sexy, really. It is so sexy watching you sink deeper and deeper into submission. I love watching you get on your knees before me and just completely surrender yourself. Offering yourself to me as a tribute. It's perfect how you do it so seemingly without effort, showing me your willingness to serve and obey."

"It's never required much effort to submit to you," he said.

"It's almost funny to think of it now," Violet said. "Full confession, when I first saw you, I thought only in terms of straddling you. Just shoving my pussy in your face. That was really as far as I'd planned ahead. You were going to lick me, and then I was going to ride your tongue while I sat on your face. I knew I was going to make an entire evening of it. Now, I admit it was spur of the moment. I'd only just met you, but I decided right then and there that I was going to come on your face, you know, however many times. But like I said, that was all I was interested in. I probably assumed that was going to be it. Maybe I didn't know how good you'd be, because at first, it was just that. I climbed off of you, thinking I'd gotten what I wanted you for, so now we were done. Then it kind of tickled something in the back of my mind. I kept thinking about how sexy you were while I was coming on your face. So, I made sure it would happen again. Soon, as it turned out. The next night you were right where I wanted you. Maybe it was an obsession at first. I know that for a while I just thought about you exclusively between my thighs. That was the image I had of you, the way you looked when you were licking my pussy. Truth be told, I still think of you that way, but it took on a different meaning when I realized how much I actually needed it from you."

"Thank you, Violet," Theo said. "I was raised to think of my value in terms of my service and support of female authority. And it's pretty much the best thing in my life to be allowed to serve you."

"I always get the giggles when I think about you growing up, a young Theo learning to be a good boy," she said, laughing.

He smiled in response.

"When did you get your first chastity cage?" she asked.

"When I first started getting erections," he replied.

"I remember when my brother, Cary, was given his first chastity cage," she said.

"It's kind of a big deal," Theo said. "It's like this coming-of-age sort of thing. It's this new, grown-up kind of responsibility. I remember we'd make fun of the boys who hadn't gotten one yet. Of course, we all knew, since we'd be changing clothes for gym and taking showers and all that."

"Did you have a locker room when you were younger?" Violet asked. "I mean, you have one now."

"Without a door," Theo said.

"Right, but I know that in many places, the boys' locker room itself was simply done away with," she said.

"No, we weren't allowed a locker room," Theo said. "For obvious reasons."

"Right," Violet said. "Did the female students ever watch the boys?"

"I guess, yeah," Theo replied. "They had every right to watch, so it didn't really register. Plus, our gym teacher, Ms. Colton, she'd have an eye on us the whole time. We just tried to be quick about it."

"Yeah, we didn't have a locker room for the boys at my school either," Violet said. "We became accustomed to seeing boys undressed. It didn't seem unusual, really. It was different for them, for sure, but it made sense that they, the boys, I mean, had a separate set of rules to govern them."

"I imagine you would have been a fairly remarkable young woman," he replied. "You still are, of course."

Violet smiled.

"You know, because of my body type, I developed early," Violet said. "It kind of scrambled the boys' brains," she added, laughing at the memory. ""Even back then my butt was really big. Super big. It made the boys literally drool when I'd wear anything tight. Which I did, probably just to make their little locks feel tight. They'd been so conditioned to treat women with greater respect, but their little hormones were going crazy. And it had been drilled into them that their urges were to make them more amenable to submission. They were driven to kneel before me, and things like that. It was really kind of embarrassing with these boys wanting to treat me like their queen, or whatever. So, I'd amuse myself with them. Couldn't help it, really. It was fun. It sounds mean, but I couldn't feel bad about boys being assigned their position when I'd see how readily they'd allow me to do anything I wanted to them. They'd kneel and beg with such sincerity. I didn't even have to be nice to them. In fact, if I happened to feel like being cruel, they'd get so turned on and twice as submissive."

"I can't imagine them being able to resist you," Theo replied.

"Well, like any young woman, I was curious," Violet said. "I knew I that I had certain advantages, maybe they could be called privileges, that boys did not have. We all knew it, my friends and I, and we talked about it. We could see that the boys were treated differently. Appropriately, we thought, because they had limitations. Not only were there limits placed upon them in the way they were to behave, but they had natural limitations as well. They simply couldn't do certain things the way we could. So, we understood why the boys had to be treated differently. We knew why they weren't allowed the same privileges we enjoyed. They had to earn what privileges they'd be allowed, and it clearly wasn't easy for them given their natural inabilities. In a way I think we felt sorry for them because we could see the struggle they were going to have. But we also felt that really, they'd only gotten what they deserved. If a boy was punished for his own actions, we had to admit that he only had himself to blame. The rules were clear enough."

Violet thought for a moment.

"Do you ever watch porn?" she asked. "I mean you know, when you were younger?"

"Generally, no," he replied. "It's," he began, then gestured toward his chastity device. "It's too restrictive for that kind of thing."

"Oh, right," she said, amused by the sight of his caged semi-erection. "It would just be frustrating for you, I guess."

"Yes," he replied.

"I was so impressed when I saw how small your chastity device is," she said. "You looked like you were restrained good and hard. I love that look. It was so small and so tight that it made me wet. Which meant that I had to have you lick me, so I straddled your face then and there. And you have amazing skills in using your tongue, so I decided to keep you around."

She kissed him softly.

"But wait, you said generally, no," Violet said. "So that means sometimes, yes."

"Right," Theo said. "When I was younger, you know. I guess I thought it might be educational. I'd watch porn videos where it would be, like, an hour or something of a boy going down on a woman," Theo said.

"Did you notice that pretty much all of the images you were seeing had a boy licking a woman's pussy?" she asked.

"Well, yeah," he replied. "That was what it was. Or is, I guess. I'd see the websites with just photos, and they'd be stills from the videos, or photoshoots, maybe. Each of them would show a variation of a woman wearing clothing or maybe not, but the boy would always be naked, and he'd have his face between her thighs. The focus of each image was the apparent pleasure the female was feeling in the moment. So every image was some really beautiful pose or position or a different take on a situation where you'd see a woman's pussy being licked. Worshipped."

"I like it that the boy is always completely naked," she said.

"Yeah, but that's what they do in porn, right?" he asked, laughing gently at the thought.

"And the women would be however," she said. "Maybe nude, maybe dressed."

"But always really beautiful, I thought," he replied.

"Yeah, I thought it was nice to see all shapes and sizes of women being serviced by all these naked boys," she said. "I imagine it actually was instructional for you."

"Yes, definitely," he said. "I saw how there were as many different approaches to satisfying a woman's body as there were women's bodies."

Violet bit her lower lip as she contemplated the thought of his education, thinking about a younger Theo watching and learning how to lick pussy. She smiled at the thought.

"I actually do watch porn," Violet said. "Not all the time, just, you know, whenever. You know what I think is so hot? You know that website where you can watch a boy fuck himself in the ass with a dildo? Like, big ones? The dildos, I mean," she said, laughing.

"I think so," Theo replied. "They have these really massive, big dildos that they'll mount to a wooden chair or something like that and the boy sits on it?"

Yeah, it's called Slow Ride," she said. "The boys will take every inch of it, then he starts riding it. It's way more fun than it should be," Violet said, giggling at the thought. "The boys always look so cute. The expression on their face, you know? The boy is always like, oh my god, oh my god as their asshole is being stretched wide to take the enormous girth of one of those super-massive dildos. And then they have to take it all, all the way down. I so get off on watching the look of shock on the boy's face when he realizes how huge it is, and now he has to not just take it in the ass, but he has to actually start fucking himself while the audience watches him do it."

"Um, OK," Theo replied, unsure of how to react to the information.

Violet placed her middle finger into her mouth, making it wet with her saliva, then reached down and slid it deep inside Theo's asshole. He relaxed his body in response.

"So, what do you think about auditioning to be on Slow Ride?" she asked.

"The website?" he asked in response.

"Yes, idiot, the website," she said, giggling at his reply.

"Do you want me to?" he asked.

"Wow, Theo, do you want the belt?" she asked. "I ask a question, you reply with a question, then another question and I haven't even gotten a response yet."

She reached down with her other hand and wrapped it tightly around his balls.

"What. Do you think?" she asked.

"I would be terrified and happy to do that if you want," he replied.

"I want," she said.

She squeezed his balls in her hand and pushed her finger harder into his ass.

"I want that, and I want you to take it deep and hard," she said. "I wonder how much you can handle. They have really big, fat dildos. Like a forearm. I want to see you take one of those in your cute little butt."

She began rhythmically squeezing his balls while she slid her middle finger in and out of his ass.

"You'll look so fucking naked," she said. "I will get so wet watching you fuck yourself with everyone watching. Maybe I'll write my name across your chest so that everyone will know you're my property."

Theo gasped at the sensation of Violet's grip while penetrating him.

"Thank you, Violet," he said in a breathy voice. "Thank you for allowing—"

"Hmmm, yeah, down," she said, pulling her hands free to push Theo downward to lick her pussy.

She held his head in place and placed her feet on his lower back, thrusting her hips against his mouth while he used his tongue to the best of his ability. He drew each of her labia into his mouth, between his lips, licking and kissing them in adoration. Violet always felt as though Theo's skill was in making clear he had no intention of ever stopping when he lavished attention on her pussy. She felt as though he would lick and suck and kiss her there forever if he could. Theo's tongue encircled her clit while the tip slid in between her clitoral hood and her clitoris. Violet shivered with pleasure at the sensation.

She thought about Theo, stripped naked and mounting a giant, ass-dominating dildo while she watched. It didn't take long for her fantasy to push her over the edge, making her cum hard on his face.

Chapter 15

"Hey, I'm going home again this weekend," Violet said while walking to the cafeteria.

"Oh yeah?" Teya asked. "What, does Theo not know how to do laundry?"

Violet laughed.

"Of course he does," she replied. "And no, I'm not just going home to do laundry. Speaking of which, at what point did you decide on that outfit?"

"This?" Teya asked. "How dare you. It's my brilliant fashion choice."

Violet laughed. Teya was wearing a pair of cutoff shorts, and a thin piece of cotton T-shirt material tied across her breasts, which was pale pink and practically see-through.

"It's a choice, I'll give you that," Violet replied. "I'm kidding, for fuck's sake, you look gorgeous in anything. Maybe I'm just jealous because I don't think I could cover my nipples with that, let alone my tits."

"Are you trying to small-titty shame me?" Teya asked.

"Oh my god, of course not," Violet said. "I've told you a million times I'm jealous of your perfect little body."

"OK, as long as you recognize its perfection," Teya said with a smile.

"So anyway, Theo is going to be coming home with me, which will be interesting. He'll meet the family, and I promised my neighbor I'd stop by and let her meet him as well."

"Ooh, that's serious," Teya said. "Meeting the folks. And the weird neighbor lady."

Violet laughed.

"How did you decide that my neighbor lady is weird?" Violet asked.

"Just sounds more fun that way," Teya said.

* * *

When Violet and Theo pulled up in front of her house, she paused and turned toward him.

"OK, this is the house where I became the fabulous person that I am," she said with a twinkle in her eye. "Where I learned how to strap naked butts and dominate cute, sweet boys like you. So, show some respect."

She leaned over and kissed him.

"Why, of course," he replied.

"Shush!" she said, raising her index finger in front of her lips.

"OK, it's—"

"Shsh!" she said.

He smiled, amused that he could see that she was a bit nervous. He'd never seen her be nervous before.

She led him into the house.

"Hello!" Violet called out from the foyer of the house.

"Oh, Violet, honey, we're in here," her mother replied.

Violet led Theo into the kitchen, where her mother was sitting on one of the barstools that had been placed along one side of the kitchen island. Violet's father was on his knees, painting her mother's toenails.

"Oh, hey, Mom, Dad," Violet said. "This is Theo," she said, bringing Theo forward.

'Why hello, Theo," Violet's mother said. "You may call me Veronica."

"Mom?" Violet murmured. "Her name is Rachel," Violet whispered to Theo.

"And this is my husband, his name is Garrett, though everyone calls him Gary," her mother said.

"Well, at least that one is correct," Violet whispered. "OK, I've got to go introduce him to the rest of the family," she announced.

"It's a pleasure to meet you, Veronica, Gary," Theo said as she whisked him away.

"Right, so that's my parents," Violet said as they walked downstairs to the lower level of the house.

Violet stopped by the laundry room, where her brother Cary was sorting clothing to be washed.

"Hey, Cary," she said, then had to hang on to Theo to keep herself from falling to the floor, laughing hysterically. "What the holy dick, Cary!" she exclaimed. "Is this a special occasion?"

Cary was wearing a pair of black, see-through, thong panties, a pair of sheer, black, thigh-high stockings, and a pair of black patent leather shoes with a five-inch heel. He also wore a shirt whose design had become popular among boys as of late, which was a long-sleeved blouse made of white, transparent fabric that had a collar he'd buttoned up to the neck. The tails of the shirt ended at his upper chest, just above his nipples, leaving his upper body mostly exposed.

"It's," Cary began, blushing, "it's because Isabella said so. She wants to see me dressed up for her."

"Well, good job, Cary," Violet said, laughing. "Theo, this is my brother, who's apparently got a hot date with a lovely young woman in the neighborhood. And bitch-boy, this is Theo, who's my sweet, submissive servant boy."

"For whatever it's worth, my opinion is that you've done a really nice job with your outfit," Theo said. "The whole black-and-white look is sharp. Good luck."

"Thank you, Theo," Cary replied. "It's nice to meet you. Violet has never brought home—"

"Lalalala!" Violet blurted out, making a frantic gesture.

Cary halted.

"Well then, we should let my little brother get on with his, um," she said, "when is this date?"

"Oh, right," Cary replied. "She wants me to come over this afternoon."

"Woah, this afternoon?" Violet asked. "Will you be ready in time?"

"That's why I'm trying to be quick with my chores," Cary replied.

"Are you nervous?" she asked.

"Yes," he admitted.

"Good. You should be," Violet said. "Just think about what a privilege it is to be offered the opportunity to submit to a woman like Isabella."

"I understand, Violet," Cary said. "Thank you."

* * *

"I want to see you wearing a pair of heels," Isabella had told Cary the week before. "Five-inch heel, I'm thinking. Really slutty, with a pair of cute panties. And thong panties, really tiny. Too tiny. What do you think, Cary, could you do that for me? Are you up for the challenge?"

"Yes, Miss Isabella," he'd replied, not knowing if what he'd said was true.

"Good," she said. "You will purchase the following: a pair of platform high-heeled shoes. You may need to special order a pair that fit the size of your feet. Then you will purchase a pair of thigh-high stockings. You may select a pair that depend on the use of a garter belt, or you may choose a pair that has an adhesive lining that helps them remain in place without support.

They should be sheer, so that your bare legs remain visible when wearing them. The entirety of your body will be shaved, smooth and hairless, of course."

She paused, enjoying the image in her mind.

"The pair of panties is, perhaps, the most important of your purchases, as you will want this item to satisfy a number of criteria," she continued. "The most important aspect of this item is that it is the smallest amount of fabric necessary to cover you. Tiny is the operative attribute. They should provide the bare minimum of coverage. Like I said, a thong style is appropriate. Thin, delicate straps for the waistband are preferable. The pair of panties should be decidedly feminine. Sheer, or see-through in the front panel is preferable. No, required. Lace, tiny bows, or similar accoutrements are encouraged. I'm looking for something one might use the words "precious" or "adorable" to describe. In short, the less they look as though they will fit you, the better," Isabella said, and her smile looked a bit predatory.

"Your entire outfit should be a bit more revealing than you prefer," she said. "When you are wearing your little outfit, it should feel like you are wearing nothing."

**

Cary took his time in shaving the entirety of his body. Then he put on the panties, the stockings, the shoes, and the see-through shirt. He stood in front of the full-length mirror to examine himself, making sure that everything was in place. He had been told that his butt was one of his best features and that he should show it off. He turned and looked at himself in profile. The heels on his feet and the thong panties worked to his advantage, making his bare butt look prominently available. He turned back to face himself and saw that his chastity cage was fully visible beneath the sheer fabric of his panties.

As it was a special occasion, he wondered if his mother might allow him to wear the key to his lock on a necklace. He had seen some boys do that and though it looked scandalous for any male to display his own key, he thought it would be an attractive addition to his outfit. He wondered if his mother would agree.

"Well, look at you," his mother said. "You look very nice. Are you excited about your date?"

"I'm nervous, but yeah, I am," he replied. "And thank you. But I have one little thing I wanted to ask for," he said cautiously.

"What is that?" she asked.

"You know how some boys will wear their own key on a necklace?" he asked.

"Well, it's generally not "their" key, but I am generally aware," she said. "And what does that have to do with you?"

"I was hoping to do that," he said. "Wear it, I mean. I promise that I won't use it." He was emphatic with his delivery, hoping that she might decide to trust him.

"Well, then what is the purpose of you wearing it?" she asked. "Are you trying to project the idea that it is yours to offer?"

"No," he said, though he was unsure if that was true.

"Good, because it is not," his mother replied.

"It's that it just reinforces the fact that I'm locked like I should be, and I wouldn't dream of using it, I promise. I just wanted to look my best. Please?" he asked finally.

"I suppose it will help you in the way that you say," she admitted. "I don't think you need it, but if you promise not to try to use it, then I guess I can let you wear it."

"Thank you," he replied, doing his best to sound grateful without sounding too excited.

She gave him the key on a short necklace which he fastened around his neck.

"I don't have to tell you to be on your best behavior, right?" she asked.

"I know, I will," he replied.

Cary made the short walk across the street and down three houses to Isabella's house. He was nervous about being dressed the way that he was in public, but there were few people out in the neighborhood. He did encounter one of his neighbors, Ms. Kiernan, who was out for a walk with her dog.

"Why, Cary, you look attractive today," she said warmly. "I imagine you've an important event? Or perhaps a date?"

"Yes, Ms. Kiernan," Cary replied, stopping to speak with her as manners would dictate. "I have a date."

"How nice," she said. "Well, remember to be pay attention to the little things. Women like thoughtful young boys."

"Thank you," Cary replied.

* * *

Isabella was surprised and impressed by how Cary's choice of high-heeled shoes and tiny panties not only met but exceeded her expectations. She felt that the little outfit not only looked good on his tight, muscular body, but it actually looked embarrassing. Isabella felt that this was the high bar of accomplishment in boys' apparel, the point where it seemed impossible that the all-but-naked boy in question appeared as though he couldn't possibly not be embarrassed to wear what he was wearing.

"So fucking adorable!" she exclaimed, expressing her approval.

She laughed with delight at the vision of Cary standing before her. He seemed as though he would look less naked if weren't wearing what he was wearing.

"Such a cute, tiny pair of panties, and the shoes, I so love the way they look on you," she said. "So tall and your legs and butt looks so tight and sexy. Like you're on display. Little boy toy in your cute, tiny panties, little dick locked up securely—"

Isabella paused.

"Is that what I think it is?" she asked, spying his key on a chain around his neck.

"Yes, it's the key to my chastity cage," he replied.

"So naughty," she said, with a mischievous look in her eye. "Wearing the key on a chain like you're pretending it belongs to you. It's super cute and so sexy. I love it."

"I promised my mother I wouldn't use it," he said.

"I'm sure you did," she said as she stepped closer to him. "However, I've made no such promise."

She lifted the necklace from around his neck, then pulled his panties down in front and slid the key into the lock. She unlocked the device, and slowly worked it free of his body. Cary stood at attention as she unlocked him, a feeling of nervousness flooding his mind. He was unsure of what he should do in the situation, deciding that submission required him to do as he was told. So he remained still. She held his panties down in front as she examined him.

"Your little penis is so cute," Isabella said. "What are you, like, four inches or something?"

"It's just over five—" Cary began.

"OK, rule one, never contradict me," Isabella said curtly, her finger in his face. "Say that it is four inches."

"It's um," he said, "it's four inches."

"That wasn't so hard, was it?" she asked, then she laughed. "Actually, it *is* pretty hard. You and your three-inch penis, you definitely need to know your place. I wanna flick it hard and watch it react." She laughed, watching him blush in reaction.

Isabella drew her middle finger back with her thumb, then flicked the tip of Cary's penis.

She laughed at the sight of it practically vibrating in response.

"That's my favorite thing about the male body," she said. "When you boys get so hard that it's like a spring, and just a little flick will make it quiver."

Isabella examined him for a moment longer, then pulled his panties up over his erection.

"I can see the tip of your erect penis pressing against your panties," she said with a devious smile. "Admit that it should be under my heel. Think about how good it would feel to have your little penis right where it should be, getting squeezed so tight between the heel of my foot and the hardwood floor."

"Yes, Isabella," he replied.

"OK, so far, so good," she said. "Now, let's see a little walk. Why don't you walk to the far wall. Like it's a little catwalk."

Cary did his best to walk confidently in the high-heeled shoes. He was grateful that he'd spent time practicing.

"Acceptable," Isabella said. "Now do a little spin, revealing your cute little erection stuffed into your panties and walk back to me."

He walked toward her, noticing her posture. She had her hands on her hips, projecting an attitude of amused judgment. It was intimidating for Cary, but he tried to do as he'd practiced, walking a center line, toe-heel, toe-heel.

"Adorable," she said, and the smile she had in reaction made Cary feel a surge of pride in himself. "Now, let's try something more difficult."

She showed Cary what he recognized as a butt plug, only he'd never seen one the size Isabella was holding in her hand. She laughed.

"The look on your face!" she exclaimed. "That's so sexy, I can see that you're really intimidated, and you should be. Come on, this is a monster. But then I can also see that oh-so-attractive look of resolve. The way that you boys try to look tough. It's really adorable seeing a boy try to look all tough when he's wearing a pair of little panties. All right, turn around and stick out your ass."

Cary complied, presenting his ass to Isabella.

"Pull the thong to one side," she said. "Two hands, spread your ass for me like a slut."

Cary spread his cheeks and took a deep breath. He felt the lubricated tip of the butt plug against his asshole.

"This is going to feel like, well, like a massive butt plug violating your ass, to tell the truth. But you already knew that. What you might not know is that it is going to feel like a hilariously perfect victory for me, watching your asshole get stretched to its limit and witnessing your surrender to its domination of your cute little butt. She took her time, watching

Cary submit to its full and unrelenting penetration until he'd taken it to the hilt.

"That's perfect," she said, "now let's see you do your cute little walk."

Cary did his best to perform his catwalk routine with the enormous plug in his ass.

"Ha-ha, I can't decide what I like seeing more," Isabella said, "how well you're able to hide how deeply your ass is being violated, or how obvious it is. Or is it the fact that you still have a tiny erection in your panties?"

She laughed joyously at the sight of Cary blushing with humiliation as he made his spin and walked back toward her.

"Come here, my little supermodel," she said.

She took each of his nipples in between her thumb and forefinger and pinched them firmly as she pulled him toward and gave him a kiss.

"Look, I think it would be in your own self-interest if I gave you a little spanking across the balls, don't you think?" Isabella asked. "Just a quick little corrective measure, nothing too extreme. Just something to put you in your place, a reminder, really. Don't you agree?"

Cary felt a surge of fear. His mouth went dry.

"Yes," he replied, which he'd realized was always the safest answer. But he also realized that he meant it. She was always right, and in this instance, it was no different, regardless that it meant she would be punishing his balls.

"Good, I appreciate that you understand your need to surrender," she said. "Get on your knees and elbows now. We're going to do this from behind, so spread your knees wide. Rotate your hips and offer them to me. I want to see from your position that you recognize your place in this little ritual. You are going to receive the gift of my training, so I want to see willing consent and an anticipation of the gratitude you will feel as a result."

Cary assumed the position. Isabella retrieved a short leather paddle then sat down beside him. She used her fingertips to stroke his balls in a way that sent shivers through his body.

"Think about how proud you will be to say that you've been trained to serve me," she said. "It will be very impressive to anyone who hears it. It will communicate to them that you have been put through your paces, and everyone knows I do not tolerate disobedience. It will show them that you have demonstrated the ability to subjugate yourself to female authority far beyond what it expected of you. All boys submit, but you will have shown the capacity for going much, much further and deeper into submission. You will have quite obviously demolished your own ego."

She slowly caressed his balls. She did so gently, while still projecting an aura of menace.

"A cowardly, disobedient pig will allow his fear to control his body, whereas an obedient boy will surrender without question, and accept his trial of punishment," she said. "I'm looking forward to finding out which of the two you are. Say that you owe it to me to have your balls punished," she said.

"Please," he said in a voice that was practically a whimper, showing his desperation.

"That's a good start," she said. "Please, Isabella, please punish my balls. Say it."

He took a deep breath, then exhaled, his body trembling in fear.

"Please, Isabella," he said.

"Uh-huh," she said. "Please Isabella what?"

"Please," he said, "punish my balls."

"Nice," she said. "Good job. You did it. That wasn't so hard, was it? Just think about how good it's going to be when I let you lick my pussy. And think about how proud you will feel when I tell my friends all about how you submitted to having your balls spanked. They'll be so impressed when I tell them you begged for it. Now, it's not just going to be once. And I want to hear you beg for each and every one. Understand?"

"Yes, Miss," he replied.

She took ahold of him by the back of his head and brought his face around to kiss him. Her lips were soft yet insistent, meeting his with an expectation of his submission to her. Her breasts pressed against his body. Her tongue delved into his mouth briefly before she pulled away.

"Do you think you can do that?" she asked. "Beg with sincerity?"

He felt overwhelmed in the moment, her having kissed him being just one of the things that made him all but swoon. She laughed.

"Of course you can," she said.

She sat up and held the short leather paddle against his balls.

"Say it again," she said. "Say please, Isabella, please punish my balls."

"Please, Isabella," Cary said, "please punish my balls."

"Hmmm, I just love the sight of a boy about to get his balls spanked," Isabella said, her voice somewhere between sultry and domineering. "You all look so cute like that. You get this delicious fear in your eyes. Hmmm," she said, stroking his balls with her fingertips. "I can't imagine not having boys submit to me on a regular basis. I will have you continue to serve me after this, you know. I see some potential in you. But first, I want to see how you pass this little test."

She drew the paddle back, ready to unleash the first stroke, then held it for a moment, watching the expression on his face. His body tensed in response.

"That's pretty, you look like you're ready for it," she said. "And now it's time to give you what you've begged for so sweetly.

She took ahold of his balls and held them in a commanding grip. The heel of her hand was pressed against the massive butt plug. Then she spanked him with the paddle, which made him gasp, then moan in pain. Isabella laughed with delight.

"Brilliant," she said. "That was such a nice reaction. I bet you want it again, don't you?"

Cary had to sink deep within himself to find the courage to submit, to lower himself in supplication in the face of fear. "Yes," he replied, though the word was lost in the moment as she swung the paddle and slapped him squarely across the balls again.

"Oh, that was nice," she purred. "It makes my pussy so wet to watch a boy get what he has coming to him, and I can tell it really hurts."

"Speaking of my perfect, deliciously dripping wet pussy, I think you should show your gratitude for my having put you in your place, don't you think?" Isabella asked.

"Yes, Miss," Cary replied, "thank you."

"Oh, but not yet," she said. "I know how much you boys love being put in your place. You respect women who give you the punishment you deserve. And you deserve more, don't you, Cary?"

He began to speak in response, not knowing if he'd have a voice with which to answer. "Yes, Miss Isabella," he replied.

"Oh, that's so nice to hear your voice tremble like that," Isabella said. "You're being brave, aren't you?"

She moved the paddle in circles, gently caressing his balls.

"I so appreciate boys like you being brave," she said. "Because that means you're scared."

She pulled the paddle back.

"Now don't flinch," she said. "You'll get two for flinching."

She spanked him across the balls, and it took everything Cary had to offer to remain in place and accept the sensation of pain as a gift to guide his descent into submission.

"Impressive," Isabella said. "Now my little bitch-boy has earned himself the right to worship my pussy."

Isabella laid back on the carpet and pulled Cary's face between her thighs. Her dress had ridden up, exposing her naked pussy, and Cary had his tongue in service of her clit within moments.

"That's perfect," Isabella said. "Show me your appreciation for my having handed you your balls, Cary. I mean bitch-boy."

Chapter 16

It was early afternoon in the kitchen of the home where Violet had spent her childhood. Theo stood before the sink, washing the dishes from lunch. A warm shaft of light streamed in through the window above the sink, which was part of what had Theo feeling relaxed and happy. He looked out the window as he scrubbed the dishes in soapy water. There was an expanse of green lawn in the backyard, and he saw that there was what was left of an old piece of rope tied to a thick, practically horizontal branch of the largest tree. He imagined there must have been a swing, perhaps an old tire swing, hanging there for Violet to play on when she was young. He smiled at the thought.

He was close to being finished with the dishes when Violet's mother walked into the kitchen and stood leaning against the edge of the counter, observing him for a moment.

"I'm guessing that my daughter finds your obedience acceptable," she said in a friendly manner, "which is a remarkable achievement, really. She has very high standards, I've noticed. You must have done something right to be on her arm, so to speak."

Theo smiled at what he realized was a significant compliment.

"She makes it easy," Theo said with a shrug.

"Are you sure we are talking about the same woman?" her mother asked. "My daughter is not in the habit of making anything easy. I say that as the highest praise, of course."

Theo smiled, and said, "I mean that I have no trouble being motivated to do as she commands. It's easy to submit to a woman as attractive as she is. And I mean attractive in the broadest sense. Everything about her draws me toward her."

"Yes," she said, "yes, I suppose. Interesting. I understand the two of you are going over to meet Sonia?"

"Ms. Taylor?" Theo asked. "Yes, that is what Violet said."

"I heard my name," Violet said, walking into the kitchen.

"I was just mentioning to your boy Theo that the two of you are planning to go over to Sonia's house," her mother said. "You'll want to keep an eye on this one," she said gesturing toward Theo. "Sonia has an appetite for beautiful young boys."

"Well, not to worry, Theo is mine, so nothing will change that," Violet said. "Plus, she has her new boy toy to play with."

"Who is that?" her mother asked.

"Aaron," Violet replied. "You remember Aaron, right?"

"Oh my, he's just a baby," her mother said.

"He's eighteen, so not really," Violet said.

"Goodness, they grow up so fast," her mother said.

"Anyway, come on, Theo. We should head over before my mom makes up more weird things to say."

* * *

"I will say that she's very sweet and nice and mom-like," Theo said as they walked along the sidewalk towards Ms. Taylor's house.

"Mom-like?" Violet asked. "Does that mean very peculiar?"

"Sometimes," Theo said with a shrug.

"Weird. Anyway, we're here," Violet said as they turned the corner and arrived at the entry to a spacious lawn with a formidable estate looming above.

"So close," Theo said. "Oh my god."

"Yeah, rich woman, big house," Violet said, amused by his reaction.

"Why, hello, dear," Sonia greeted Violet warmly once they'd made their way to the back of the house. "This must be your charming young servant boy."

"Yes, this is Theo," she said. "Theo, this is Ms. Sonia Taylor."

"Please, call me Mistress Sonia," she said.

"It is a pleasure to meet you, Mistress Sonia," Theo said. "You have a beautiful home."

"But of course," Sonia said.

Violet took a seat on the sofa, and Sonia observed closely as Violet allowed Theo a seat next to her.

"So, what does your young man study at school?" Sonia asked.

"He is a nursing student," Violet replied. "If I get sick, he'll have the right skillset."

"Very clever of you," Sonia said.

"Does he talk back to you when you've given him an order?" Sonia asked.

"Rarely," Violet said.

"Are you quick to punish him when he has done so?" she asked.

"I do my best to be consistent with him," she said. "But he's so cute."

"I completely relate to that," Sonia said. "But as I'm sure you know, consistency is important with them. I understand that you won't want to be obligated all the time. Ideally you will get him to understand that it is always in his best interest to follow your command without comment. They can be pretty when they're obedient, and such a pleasure when they consistently offer submission. But the male gender will tend to reveal limitations in the ability to listen and follow directions. They may be trained to respond better, but they will still need correction from time to time."

"We definitely spend time focused on his training," Violet said.

"I generally feel that the female and the male should work together to find what feels most natural for her while delivering her message in the most direct manner," Sonia said. "Ideally, it will be relatively effortless for her to visit upon his body an immediate correction. Every boy is different, you know. In a new relationship, I recommend a couple try out any number of methods in trying to discover what will communicate to the male the message she wishes to communicate to him. For some, it will be a sharp, stinging pain. For others, a hard beating is in order. This should be fun for her to explore. Apply a variety of sensations to his body to see what he reacts to most significantly."

Violet smiled.

"He is pretty responsive when I apply the belt," Violet said.

"So, Theo," Sonia said, "Let me ask you your thoughts about the discipline you receive at Violet's hand?"

"I will admit to having been afraid, at first, of facing my own need to be given correction," Theo said. "But Violet has been so amazingly patient with me, and supportive of my eventual acceptance of my place in regard to her. I'm not sure that someone less loving and kind wouldn't have given up on my training. But she showed resolve in getting me to the point where I can now fully embrace the transformative power of corporal punishment at her hand."

"That's very sweet of you, honey," Violet said. "And he has come a long way. When I give him the look, he knows it's in his best interest to assume the position without hesitation. And when I ask him what he deserves as penalty, his answer will not only be sincere, but it will, on occasion, impress me. He has come to understand that beyond just being for the purpose of discipline, his punishment is also a tribute to be paid to me. An offering that displays his willingness to suffer for me as a show of respect."

"Do you feel that when you give him a reminder by way of the strap, or the whip, or the paddle, that it puts him in the right mindset to obey in the way you not only want, but need?" Sonia asked.

"If you'd asked me at the beginning of last semester, my answer might have been different, but now I would say yes," Violet said.

"I would like to hear him answer the same question," Sonia said. "When she puts you in your place by way of testing the limits of your tolerance for pain, does it put you in the right mental space with respect to your relationship to her?"

"Yes, absolutely," Theo replied. "I am so enamored of her to begin with, and after she's given me an opportunity to pay penance for my failures, I feel an overwhelming love and adoration for her."

"Well, I will say that I like everything I'm hearing," Sonia said. "And he's such a pretty young thing. Well-built and all of that. I approve."

"I'm glad to hear it," Violet said. "I agree."

She gently elbowed Theo.

"Thank you, Mistress Sonia," he said.

"He's much more attractive when he's on his knees," Violet said.

"They really do look their best that way," Sonia said. "Their bodies are uniquely formed to be displayed in that manner. Showing off the locked chastity device. And with the arms up and with the hands behind the head, open position, so you can see everything. That suits them perfectly, the way their bodies look when they assume that pose and hold it, not moving until given instruction. Respectfully silent, of course. Eyes down. The position itself keeps boys out of trouble, and it shows off their obedience too. It's so attractive to see a boy who is proud of his own submission and surrender."

"It's funny that when I was younger, I'd never really had any specific thoughts about the position," Violet said. "Boys just looked so natural in that pose that I never thought of them otherwise. It just fits their status so perfectly."

"The institution of the kneeling position for boys was part of what was instituted when we, as we called it, began *stripping the boys,*" Sonia said with a soft chuckle.

"That does sound rather suggestive," Violet said with a laugh.

"Well, yes, they were stripped of their clothes, but more importantly, their rights. We simply legislated that males had no inherent rights at first. This meant that they would have to appeal to female authority for any kind of legal protection. This helped ensure their compliance. Then, gradually, we began to allow certain of the boys to prove themselves, essentially. They'd be given certain allowances based on a proven track record of submission to female authority, which gave them the tools to prove that they could be trusted to know their rightful place."

"We've talked about it a lot," Violet said, "so I know that there were some who made the transition rather difficult for themselves. But it's sometimes hard to imagine. I mean, I ask Theo about it, and he'll say that he can't imagine his having grown up any other way. It seems that it was fairly easy for him to adjust to his reality."

"Oh, I know," Sonia said. "That's why I am so delighted with Aaron. He's never even thought of being anything other than a good, obedient servant boy. But right, like I've said before when we've talked about it, there were some for whom the humiliation was brutal," Sonia said plainly. She shrugged.

"Funny thing about it is the patriarchy didn't need to be smashed," she said. "It just needed a little prick. It deflated like an old balloon. There was nothing supporting it. Boys never had any claim to the privilege they'd enjoyed, so when they made any attempt to challenge its overthrow, they had nothing to back it up. Even its most strident supporters were chastened when they realized the truth of their own relative inferiority. They buckled under the weight of it, like they literally went weak in the knees. They fell into a genuflecting position quite naturally in recognition of their superiors."

Violet smiled, and glanced at Theo, grateful that he hadn't had to make what she felt must have been a difficult transition.

"There was this one boy," Sonia began, then paused, "well, no, there were many, but one in particular. His name was Cameron West, and he was particularly ill-suited to making the adjustment. He was, by his own admission, a true believer in male dominance, socially and otherwise. He was outspoken in support of a patriarchal system and was always on about how women were unfit for holding positions of power and authority. Anyway, he was assigned a particularly brutal series of humiliating assignments, each of which, to be fair, he himself chose over the easy path of committing himself to the gender-based system of male submission."

"So what did he have to do?" Violet asked.

"Lots of things, Sonia said, "but there was one I remember that involved something called a sling. It was like a short length of nylon rope around the balls that led to the ankles. He had to crawl, but not too quickly, because the rope was so short. Then another rope from around the balls, between the butt cheeks, up the back and tied around the neck. Again, it was so short he had to keep his head up and arch his back to lessen the pull on his neck and his balls. He had to crawl like that from one end of this really large building to the other, on a concrete floor. Moving too quickly meant the sling would pull tightly on his balls. But crawling too slowly meant he had to do it again. It was a timed exercise. He was on camera the whole time, enduring these trials publicly for entertainment."

"That sounds kind of brutal, yet hilariously entertaining," Violet said.

"Oh, he got a lot of attention at the time. Then he was cast in a pornographic film and his costar was a boy with an enormous penis, really big and all that. He had to suck off the boy, then get fucked in the ass. Rather than accept the loving guidance of female rule, he did the movie. Then another, and another, and after not too long he became one of the most in-demand and prolific porn stars, known for being paired with really well-hung boys and doing videos where he'd be simultaneously fucked in the ass and the mouth. He could deep throat like a champion. And he could take these massive boys fucking him in the ass, really drilling down. He'd be unlocked for the video, and no surprise, he had a tiny little penis. But the remarkable thing is that when he got fucked in the ass he would come. Like, no one even touched his penis, he'd just come while getting reamed up the butt. His videos always had him licking up his own cum at the end, and he'd do it so slutty, just lapping it up. He turned out to be really successful in that career."

"It's funny that you said *turned out,*" Violet said, laughing.

"Yeah, we would eventually realize that poor Mr. West was just unable to admit to himself what his true motivations were about," Sonia said. "I think he's retired by now; he kind of just disappeared."

"But as you know, there were some who started out in defiance, only to crumble before us," Sonia said. "There was one boy in particular who was having more trouble than the rest in recognizing his, as I've called them, limitations. We—my friends and I—decided we could help this one boy in learning his lesson. There were four of us, me and three of my friends, and we all agreed that this boy would benefit from our taking him and giving him an education, as we called it. We each had our own reasons, I guess. I thought he was kind of cute. He was always getting in trouble and there was something about that which intrigued me. One of my friends was purely altruistic, wanting to help him, and I know that there was an unspoken interest, a curiosity in seeing this boy in a particular way. We took him to this place we liked to go at the time, which was an area on the edge of our neighborhood behind the houses. No one went there so it was private. We would just go there and talk about stuff, you know. We took him there, and I don't remember the reason we gave him. It's possible we were completely up front with him in telling him that he needed some, as we thought of it, extracurricular instruction. But for his own personal reasons, he decided to just do as we told him to."

Sonia paused, a wistful smile on her face as she recalled the event.

"Now, we'd had a number of discussions, the three friends and I, about how best to go about it," Sonia said. "We had ultimately decided that we should get his attention right away. Put him in the right frame of mind for what would follow. So, the absolute first thing we did was to order his clothes off. We told him that for him to have any chance at success in learning what we were intending to teach him, he had to begin by showing that he was committed to learning. He needed to begin with what we thought was a significant show of obedience. We ordered his clothes off, and to his credit, he recognized that his compliance was mandatory. Off came each piece of clothing, and I still remember him blushing, his hands trembling. He was so nervous, but I think he knew we were doing him a favor, as well as the fact that it was our right to make demands because we were offering him an opportunity to educate himself. Then we spent some time just satisfying our own curiosity in looking at him."

Sonia paused for a moment.

"It was less common to see male nudity being exploited for entertainment back then," she said. "We were naturally curious. So then we began, and we'd already gotten a switch, which was a long, thin branch from a willow tree that was very strong and very flexible. It was going to leave a stinging welt if we had to use it. Funny thing is that we seriously thought we might not have to, that the possibility of it being used would be enough. I guess we had overestimated him and underestimated ourselves. We each asked him a question to test him. If we felt he was dishonest or less than forthcoming in his answer, he would get the switch across his backside. To keep him in position, should that be necessary, we had him put his arms up and his hands behind his head."

"Always a good look," Violet said.

"Oh, I adore that," Sonia said. "We asked him questions, like I said. I don't remember all of the questions, of course. But I know that we asked him if he recognized the order of gender, ours being superior to his own. He knew well enough to answer that question correctly, but we drilled down, as they say, making him reveal if he thought that was deserved and if he thought it was right that he was to treat us as the dominant gender. There he began to trip himself up a bit. It turned out that he was actually harboring some resentment that our authority was greater than his own. So, we proposed a test. We were going to quiz him on a number of things, and if he failed, then he had to submit to being whipped. Not just take it because we said so, but actually ask for it as an admission of his own failure. He readily agreed. Boys can be arrogant like that. I assume you've already guessed how that went."

"He got his bare butt whipped?" she asked.

She laughed.

"Well, that's an understatement," she replied. "He ended up having to admit to his own limitations, the result of which was that he had no other course of action but to submit to being whipped for each mistake he'd made. The first being that he'd even thought to consider himself capable of being successful in our testing his abilities. Again, to his credit, he did at least admit that he had earned himself the punishment. He asked for it graciously enough, I recall."

"So, you didn't feel the need to increase the punishment?" she asked.

"We doubled what he had suggested, of course," she replied. "But he recognized that we were right in doing so. And then we had him go up on the balls of his feet to stretch his body vertically, you know? So he's extended upward. We made it clear to him that if he failed to remain in position we would have to start over with the count. We had him count and show his gratitude for each stroke of the switch, and he quite predictably had some trouble with that. We had to start over several times before he was able to demonstrate the self-discipline we expected of him."

Sonia laughed to herself, thinking about the event, now so long ago.

"I've thought about what you'd said, that exposure to female dominant material had the effect of altering the minds of the boys who viewed it," Violet said.

"Yes, I found that fascinating," Sonia said, "And it wasn't just that the male brain could be conditioned to crave female leadership. As I've mentioned before, it was determined that exposure to material that focused on the sexually dominant female that would rewire the male brain. I thought that was a revelation. Now, it's sort of irrelevant, since all the young male has to do is observe reality."

"Speaking of reality, Theo and I should get back now," Violet said. "I've a lot of work to get done this week."

"Lovely seeing you, Violet, and meeting you, Theo," she said.
"It was very nice to meet you, Mistress Sofia," Theo replied.

* * *

When Violet and Theo arrived back at school, Violet met up with Teya, Serena, and Eliana in Serena's room, where they were discussing the upcoming punishment of Charlie Taylor.

"I'm really looking forward to it," Serena said. "Not for any reason other than it's offensive to me that this dumbass ever thought to become such a disrespectful idiot in the first place."

"I can't imagine anyone thinking they could be in a position of equality while also having a penis," Teya said. "Those two things don't go together. The penis is such a clear indication of their need to be assigned a secondary status and tightly controlled. It's beyond obvious. Just think of how stupid you'd have to be to look down and see that you have a penis and then thinking you should be in charge of anything. Or be anything other than entirely focused on obedience to anyone with a pussy."

Eliana laughed.

"You know how Rochambeau works, right?" Eliana asked.

"What?" Teya asked.

"Rock, paper, scissors," Eliana replied.

"Oh, yeah," Teya said.

"Right. Rock beats scissors, scissors beats paper, et cetera," Eliana said. "OK, so like that, but it's pussy beats penis. Every time. It's seriously really easy."

"That would make the game simpler," Teya said, laughing.

"Yeah, but the thing is that we know it's really important for boys to feel they have a purpose," Violet said. "They just have to come to understand what that purpose is. Providing support in service of female authority is the best thing for them. They're so happy in submission to a dominant female."

"I know, right?" Teya said. "It's just weird when you see boys for whom it's difficult. Like, they can't figure it out."

"I don't understand how it was ever in question," Serena said. "I've tried to imagine a different social order, one not clearly defined as female dominant, and I can't quite picture it. It's laughable that boys ever thought themselves anything but the capable servants they've been shown themselves to be. I mean, think about boys when they're dressed up in their pretty little outfits, doing their best to look all sexy while stripped down to their panties. They're so well-suited to their position. They love to compete for attention, eagerly showing their willingness to be the obedient playthings we want them to be. So, how is it that there are boys that go astray like this guy Charlie?"

"Well, I'm with you in that I'm really looking forward to him get his beating," Teya said.

Chapter 17

Charlie was brought into court, and for the first time since his detainment by Officer Fuerza, he was allowed a short white smock to wear. He was brought before the judge, Ms. Hartford, a woman whose countenance was professional and fair, but who had a reputation for being unforgiving when it came to male disobedience.

"Your having been out after curfew, along with a long list of other highly questionable circumstances, has earned you an assignment of community service," Judge Hartford said. "I have spoken with your court-appointed lawyer, Ms. Ling, and we've determined that one hundred hours is a fair judgment given the circumstances. You'll be assigned to a," the judge said, lowering her glasses to examine a document, "Ms. Sonia Taylor, who has agreed to be your signatory on your commitment each week. Be aware that your compliance will be closely monitored by the court. You will be assigned a caseworker, Ms. Ellie Turner, and you will be responsible for handing in a signed and completed worksheet each Thursday. If your worksheet is not satisfactorily signed and completed, you will be brought back here for an extension of your service. Do you understand all that you've been told?"

"Yes," Charlie replied. "Thank you, judge." It was with great restraint that Charlie resisted crying out that the judge had just assigned his ex-wife as signatory in his case. Partly, he knew that it was not in his best interest to raise the issue, and he also figured they would not see that it was a problem. His court-appointed lawyer and the judge might even be fully aware of the fact.

"You will also have been offered an opportunity to speak," the judge said. "You have expressed an interest in accepting this opportunity, is that correct?"

"Yes, Judge," Charlie said.

"As long as your statement of contrition is honest and shows that you are ashamed of and are willing to learn from your mistakes, you will be allowed to give a short speech before your punishment commences. Which brings me to . . ." she said as she flipped to the next page in her file, "your punishment will be twenty strokes of the cane. This will take place tomorrow evening, is that correct?"

"Yes, that its correct," Charlie's lawyer, Ms. Ling, replied.

"Well then, it appears we have concluded the public's business on this case," the judge concluded. "Do you have any questions, Mr. Taylor?" she asked.

"No, Judge Hartford," he replied.

She peered down at him for a moment.

"I've heard you shouldn't flex in response, that it just makes it sting more that way," she said. "I will be listening to your speech tomorrow evening. Don't make me order you back into my court."

* * *

At seven o'clock the following evening, Charlie was ushered out into a glare of lights, where a small crowd was assembled. Many of those in the audience were camera crew, there to document what would be the first public punishment and shaming in quite some time.

"We are here to present Charlie Taylor," the chief of police, Lara Winton, announced. She wore a crisp, charcoal-gray blazer, and looked confident and comfortable in front of the camera in spite of its live feed being broadcast over the internet on the local law enforcement website. "Charlie was an admitted proponent of the radical belief in equality of gender," Chief Winton continued, "who had worked to upend the authority of state officials, law enforcement, and local entities whose purpose is to serve the greater good. He also endeavored to radicalize others in his beliefs and had developed plans to attempt to disable various institutions of public service and general welfare. He is here today, having come to an awareness of how misguided and dangerous his thoughts and actions were, for the purpose of renouncing his ideology and accepting a punishment for those actions. He has expressed his hope that his words, and his display of maturity in accepting his penalty with grace, will be an example to others who might be similarly misguided in their thinking. We commend him for having made the right decision in voluntarily submitting to this punishment.

We will not, however, allow that to cause us to be lenient. He will receive twenty strokes of the cane. This might not sound severe, but I can assure you that most people would be unable to endure more than three. To speak plainly, the punishment will render him unable to do anything more than crawl at best, which he will be allowed to do once his punishment has been delivered."

At that point, Charlie Taylor was brought forward into the harsh glare of the lights and made to stand before the audience. He was wearing his police-issued chastity cage, and a look of contrition. He also looked fearful of what punishment he was going to receive, but he maintained what he hoped was a look of bravery in accepting his fate.

"I am deeply ashamed of having not only given in to the misperception and delusion that the male gender is equal in standing with that of the female gender," Charlie began. "I see now that it was due to my inherent weakness, both mental and physical, that I sought the comfort of that fantasy. It was an abdication of my responsibility to learn my place. I did not realize my rightful position relative to my superiors. It was a failure to pay attention and learn what I now see as obvious. I am not the equal of the female gender. I am ashamed of my having not only embarrassed myself but having had a part in leading other males to adopt this worldview. To operate with this misguided mindset. I see now that my actions have rightfully resulted in my having earned a severe punishment. I willingly accept the punishment as penalty for my actions."

He looked down for a moment, allowing the feeling of shame and humiliation to course through his exposed and all-but-naked body.

"I admit that I was, at one point in my life, a misguided ally in gender equality," he continued. "I thought it progressive of me to think of women as being equal. I have come to realize how clueless I was in this, and it's embarrassing to think now that I once espoused such a notion. It is now apparent the fallacy that is equality, as women and men are not equal. The female gender is quite obviously superior in any number of ways. I have come to learn that it is the development of the prefrontal cortex of the male that makes me uniquely fitted to a subservient role. I have come to accept that I am ill-equipped for a leadership position, and I am best suited to following directions. Males do not have the capacity to think of the bigger picture in the way that females do. I have learned that it is in my best interest to listen when a female speaks and appreciate her guidance. When I follow directions given to me by a woman, I make better choices about my behavior."

Charlie became slightly more self-aware when he heard small sounds of approval from the audience.

"I believe that it is fear that causes men to reject this paradigm. But there is no justification for thinking that women and men must hold equal power, and we should recognize the female gender as superior, without reservation, and allow the male gender to assume its natural role of service to the female. There is no reason to reject such a model of gender status, aside from having an inflated male ego. Women are, if nothing else, naturally giving and kind as educators, and given the opportunity, will help adjust a man's ego for his own benefit. I have been the grateful recipient of a woman's natural ability to put a man in his place, and I am grateful for having been taken down in such a manner."

Charlie took a deep breath.

"Women are naturally our leaders," he said. "They deserve respect and our submission. I now offer mine, in accepting my punishment for my actions."

When he finished speaking, he assumed the position, leaning forward and placing his hands on the edge of a sturdy table that had been placed on stage for the purpose. A woman named Officer Shayla stepped up onto the stage with a long, thin cane in hand. It was sturdier than it looked by far, as Charlie was about to find out.

"We're about to find out what kind of a boy you are," Officer Shayla said.

Having never been whipped with the cane in such a ritual, Charlie was unprepared for the searing stripe across his bare ass from the first stroke of the cane. It felt like an explosion to his senses, and it would have brought him to his knees if he hadn't been securely placed in position.

He'd remembered Officer Shayla from when he'd been first brought to the police station, and she'd slid two gloved fingers into his asshole and advised him that he was going to show some hard submission. When he'd been informed that she would be the one to deliver his punishment, it was while she was in his cell, telling him as much. She made what she referred to as a very generous offer.

"I'll make the offer once," she said. "If you're smart, you'll take it."

She told him that he'd be given the opportunity to attempt to lessen the severity of his punishment if he showed her just how submissive he could be. He had to wonder what kind of punishment he would have received if he hadn't taken her up on her offer, spending upward of an hour on his knees in his cell, using his tongue to the best of his ability.

Now, he couldn't imagine her whipping him harder. As it was, the pain of each stroke of the cane, delivered with as much as a minute's anticipation between strokes, was such that he felt his resolve threatening to crumble. He gripped the table tightly, hoping he would be able to endure the remaining, excruciating strokes of the cane. By the time she was done whipping Charlie, he had all but lost the power to stand. Shayla leaned down and whispered into his ear.

"Like I said, you're going to learn to submit before we're done with you," Shayla said, then she laughed quietly before she left him to be escorted off of the stage.

Chapter 18

"So, Aaron," Sonia said, "I am going to be greatly increasing your obligations in service to me. You'll need to make sure the entirety of the interior and exterior of the house is maintained to my specifications. Obviously, I will want to be comfortable in my home, but I want to be impressed as well. I'm certain you would feel deeply ashamed if I were to notice any failure in your domestic service."

"Yes, Mistress Sonia," Aaron said.

"Hmm," she purred affectionately, placing her hand on his firmly muscled shoulder.

"To assist you, I will be assigning you the supervision of my ex-husband, Charlie, while he works off his court-ordered public service requirement.

"I will do my best, Mistress Sonia," Aaron said.

"Of course you will," she said. "I have a grocery list as well, so I want you to get on that right away."

Sonia smiled affectionately and gave him a kiss on the lips.

"Thank you, and yes, of course, Mistress Sonia," he replied.

"Good," she concluded.

Aaron took what was a very long and detailed shopping list and went to what he'd always thought of as the rich people grocery store. Sonia had given him a credit card, so he wouldn't feel nervous walking in, wondering how he could afford to buy what was on the shelves. She let him drive her BMW, which did make him a bit nervous, since it was more expensive than anything he'd been in control of before.

"What if I get in an accident?" he'd asked.

"Well, don't, because you're a rather valuable piece of machinery," she said, placing her hand on his butt and giving it a squeeze. "But I don't care about the car. I'll just buy a new one. You, precious boy, are irreplaceable." Then she'd kissed him and gave him a spank on the butt as he turned to head off to the store.

So cute, she thought as she watched him.

When Aaron took his overloaded shopping cart to the checkout, he was surprised to see an available checkout boy waiting at his check stand, offering a friendly smile. *I guess this is partly why it's so expensive,* he thought. He contrasted the experience with the grocery store he sometimes went to with his mother, where there was a long line to get to the surly, overworked checker.

"Would you like some help out to your car?" the grocery bagger asked.

"Um, well," he began to reply. He'd never had a store employee make such an offer. "I guess, sure, I guess," he responded, feeling a bit flustered.

"None of my business, really, but it looks like your owner has assigned you the grocery errands?" the grocery bagger asked on the way to the car.

"My owner?" Aaron asked.

"Oh, I meant, you know, your Mistress, or Master, or whatever she prefers to be called," he explained.

"Right," Aaron said, "but how did you know it wasn't for me?"

The grocery bagger gave him a funny look.

"Boys don't really shop here for themselves," he said. "It's just something I've observed while working at this store. Pretty much it's just boys running errands and picking up groceries for the women that run them. Of course, we have all kinds of people here, but it's, you know, kind of expensive. So usually, it's their servants who shop here. Or boy toys, or errand boys, or whatever. I don't mean to offend; I shouldn't have said anything."

Aaron laughed and opened the spacious trunk of the car to begin loading in the bags.

"It's OK, it's fine," he said. "I am proud to be a servant and a boy toy and sometimes even an errand boy to an amazing woman."

"Yeah, believe me, I'm jealous," the grocery bagger replied. "It's kind of why I got the job here, hoping that a woman might come in and decide she wanted me to load myself into the car," he said, laughing at his own joke.

"Not in the trunk, though, right?" Aaron asked.

The grocery bagger laughed again.

"Actually, I wouldn't refuse," he replied. "But sadly, the women who are rich enough to shop here *don't*. Like I said, they'll send an errand boy instead."

"Well, I'm sorry to hear it, I'll hope for the best for you," Aaron said. "And thanks so much for the help."

"Love to help, plus I get to walk outside a bit," he replied. "You take care."

When Aaron arrived back at Sonia's house, he saw that she was speaking with a young woman Aaron didn't recognize, but he did recognize Charlie, who was looking somewhat terrified while being handed over to his ex-wife's authority.

"Oh, Charlie," Sonia said, giving him a look up and down. "You're ridiculous. I told you it would be nothing but trouble for you if you kept up with your stupid crusade. Now look at you. At least you're locked up now, so that's an improvement. And it's one of those cop devices, right? I should have had you accustomed to one of those years ago."

After Aaron had put away the groceries, he came to stand beside the group, waiting quietly for Sonia to give him further instructions.

"Oh, Aaron," she said, "This is Ms. Turner, who is Charlie's caseworker, and you know Charlie, who has been remanded to my supervision for his court-ordered public service. Anyway, Charlie, as you know, I've limited time to attend to your supervision. You'll mainly be responsible to Aaron, who is, among many other things, my yard boy. He will be giving you your work assignments. If he has any issue with your compliance, he will let me know. You'll be expected to satisfactorily complete all assignments with the correct attitude and degree of diligence. Understand?"

Charlie nodded.

"Aaron, I need you to get Charlie started with his work. And when you're done with the lawn, you'll take a shower, then you can spend the afternoon attending to my more specific needs," Sonia said with a wink.

"Yes, Mistress Sonia," Aaron replied.

Sonia left to have a conversation with Ms. Turner about the details of the arrangement.

"Your main obligation, Ms. Taylor, is in making sure that Charlie performs to your satisfaction," Ms. Turner said.

"Please, call me Sonia," Sonia replied.

"Of course, Sonia, and you may call me Ellie," Ellie replied. "So, Charlie will need your signature each week. It is entirely up to you if you consent to signing off on his progress. As you have likely ascertained, Charlie may be assigned to, well, whatever you decide."

"As it should be," Sonia said.

"To tell you the truth, his lawyer, Ms. Ling, thought his penalty should be increased. The judge, Ms. Hartford, agreed, but thought it best left up to you. So Ms. Ling offered an argument in favor of the automatic extension of his service should you decide he should spend a longer amount of time under your supervision. This court determined this to be fair, so it will be up to you."

"That should be an effective motivator for Charlie," Sonia said.

"Oh, and you may be interested in knowing that Daniella, or Officer Fuerza, the officer who initially detained Charlie, she ended up getting a promotion for her handling of the case," Ellie said.

"I am delighted to hear that," Sonia said. "I met her recently and I think she's such a delightful young woman. I'm happy that everything is going well for her. Her husband, Tom, is a clever boy, and he is an employee of mine as it turns out, so after this whole event she almost seems like family to me."

"So, it sounds as though you'll have Charlie under the supervision of Aaron, I believe you called him?" Ellie asked.

"Yes," Sonia replied, "he is a rather capable boy himself."

"He is one of your servants, apparently?" Ellie asked.

"He's that and so much more," Sonia said.

"So young," Ellie said, sounding impressed.

"I highly recommend having a much younger boy," Sonia said. "For all the obvious reasons, of course. They're practically inexhaustible and beautiful to look at. But they have a more highly evolved mindset as well. They grew up with female superiority already having been firmly established, so they don't have the mental block that the older ones do. They've already been broken-in and trained. They're ready to ride," she said with a wink. "And my boy-toy Aaron is so much fun," she said, then had to laugh. "My friends ask if it isn't ridiculous having a boy his age, and I tell them it perfectly fits a woman of my standing."

"I, for one, entirely support you in having poached such a fine young specimen," Ellie replied. "And he does seem to be on point with his obedience."

"Oh, the male mind," Sonia said, "it's interesting in that it is capable of being manipulated so easily. Boys can be trained to obey your command by simply paying attention. Focus that attention. Literally hold the submissive under the power of your being entirely focused on them. They will submit to this power. They will have no choice but to submit. I only wish I knew that when I was married to Charlie."

"I'm sure that you'll know best what use to make of him," Ellie said.

"I've been playing around with the idea," Sonia said. "It would be untrue if I said there wasn't some resentment on my part for everything I went through with him. It will be rather satisfying for me to quite thoroughly put him in his place."

Ellie laughed.

"Then I will leave him in your capable hands," she said.

***

"So, you call her Mistress Sonia?" Charlie asked Aaron as they walked across the back lawn to a small shed where the gardening tools were kept.

"Yeah?" Aaron said.

"I mean, you call her *Mistress?*" Charlie asked.

"Yes," Aaron replied. "As she instructed me to call her."

"Isn't she, you know, too old for you?" Charlie asked.

Aaron stopped and his eyes narrowed.

"Is that a way of asking if I'm too young and immature?" he asked.

"No, it's just that she said," and then Charlie winced at the words he was about to speak, "she said, *attend to her needs.*"

"I'm aware of what she said, since I focus the entirety of my attention on her when she's speaking," Aaron said guardedly. "But how is that any of your business? I mean, I know she said it in front of you, but that's her right."

"No, right, of course," Charlie said. "Sorry. It's just, you know, it's an adjustment."

"No. I get it," Aaron replied. "I mean, no, I have no idea what this situation is like for you. But I see how it could be, um, difficult. May I ask how you ended up . . . ."

"Completely fucked?" Charlie asked, then almost laughed. "I don't know, it's just that everyone is different, I guess. I just had a harder time than most, maybe. You know, one thing is that I never thought a chastity cage was right. It didn't seem fair, I guess."

"You say right and fair, which sound really foreign to me as related to the privilege of being locked up," Aaron said.

"Privilege?" Charlie asked.

"Yeah, it's absolutely a privilege," Aaron said. "Maybe that's why I've been allowed to have possession of my own key. I know never to use it unless instructed to. But it is a . . . having that part of your body under lock and key is so clearly beneficial to the male mind and body. Left unrestrained, it will get you into trouble. It's so much better, it's preferable to have it under control. That women have accepted the responsibility to control that part of our anatomy is just one part of the comprehensive set of guidances they provide. A woman feels so much more at ease in her interaction with a boy if she knows he's locked tight. And denial, which, as you know, is just a necessary part of being an obedient, submissive male, is so much easier if you're locked in your device to begin with."

"I guess, I mean, I never did like having an erection that I had to repress," Charlie said. "It's embarrassing."

"Exactly. It's so much better to not get hard in the first place because you've got a really small, or inverted design," Aaron said. "I'm guessing they put you in one of the cop models when you were detained."

"Yeah, and it took some getting used to," Charlie replied. "But I suppose you're right. It did keep me from having an inappropriate, well, you know."

"Which isn't to say a woman may have her reasons for wanting to make use of your key," Aaron said. "An erection is the just male body displaying its recognition of the superiority of the female. So, she might decide to have it unlocked for her to observe. What I've learned is that when we are in the presence of a member of the dominant gender, the penis will signal its submissive status by becoming erect. It's a physical response to her natural authority. Like an offering, or a tribute. Paying respect. Which doesn't mean she is obligated to address it. Women are not required to mention their awareness of the male body's admission of its subservient status, because they have every right to expect it of us. It may be of interest to them to observe our physical body issue its confession in recognition of their natural authority, but it need not be acknowledged. She would have expected the male in question to kneel in submission to her regardless. That is her right, to expect that the male knows its place in relation to her."

"I guess that's why Sonia has you as her, um . . ." Charlie began.

"*Boy toy* is generally what she calls me," Aaron said.

"Right," Charlie said. You've got the right attitude about all of this."

"All of this?" Aaron asked.

"Yeah, I mean it's still sort of new for me," Charlie said. "The social order. And you seem to have kind of effortlessly accepted it."

"It's easy," Aaron said. "Just surrender. Having been properly trained, I can say that I truly appreciate female authority. If, as a male, you simply obey, your life will be perfect."

"Yeah, I guess," Charlie said. "When I began the process of learning my place, I guess what I felt at first was shame. Shame that I ever thought I had the right to claim equal standing with the female gender. But as I progressed in educating myself, my limitations became clearer. Having seen the world women inhabit with ease, I saw how I was incapable of operating at that level. I have come to learn that it is my place to follow, serve, and submit, whatever that might entail. I longer question female authority, but instead, I try to practice gratitude for it."

"It's as simple as that," Aaron said.

"So, I'm sure that Sonia, or I guess I should say Mistress Sonia, appreciates your mindset," Charlie said.

"My approach to submission is to be mindful of my own worst impulses," Aaron replied. "Selfishness and arrogance are two of the worst traits. Some boys feel they should get something in return for their obedience, like they are owed something. This is very damaging to their relationships with the dominant gender. The more that you surrender and give of yourself, offering all that you are capable of, the more you will get in return. The behaviors a woman might decide she dislikes, things you need to correct about yourself, you need to realize that she knows best for you and that she will take care of correcting such behavior."

"After our divorce, Sonia said that she should have been more attentive to guiding and correcting me," Charlie said.

"I've found that women will know what behaviors are detrimental to your success in serving her," Aaron said. "You can't even begin to submit if you are not going to effectively alter your behavior and become a slave worthy of her authority. But you need to start working on changing yourself. This isn't easy, but it is possible. Having someone else talk to you about your difficulty in being the ideal, submissive version of yourself can help. If you are willing to work at it, then submission can become an automatic response you no longer need to think about. The best things are never easy. Work hard, and you will be rewarded. There are some things that should hurt. Certainly, there are men who should be made to feel ashamed of their thoughts and actions. And personally, I have found a transformative power in being made to feel physical pain."

"I can attest to that," Charlie said. "I certainly got my ass handed to me during my detainment by law enforcement."

"Just keep in mind that if a woman is willing to take you on and train you to be her slave, you owe her a lot," Aaron said. "She's going to have a lot of responsibility in teaching you to not just serve, but also go way beyond. You owe her not just your attention, adoration, and respect, you also owe her your best in making it worth her while."

"I'm sure that she appreciates your attitude," Charlie said, "and obviously, your, you know, physicality."

"My physicality? You mean my physical body?" Aaron asked, sounding amused. "I tend to forget about that, to tell you the truth. I've found that most women will want you to be physically fit more than anything, which just comes from being active and doing the work. I know that it used to be that boys would try to get a large as possible because they wanted to appear dominant. They thought that their bodies, their physical size could make up for their other shortcomings. But I think it was ridiculous for them to think that way. They didn't have the mental capacity for leadership roles, so it was irrelevant for them to attempt to increase their size. When it became universally accepted, or acknowledged, really, that the male body was valued for its strength, yes, but also its adaptability, flexibility, and endurance, then it was understood that a leaner, more streamlined shape was a more desired shape for a boy."

"I should really just focus on doing the work, as you say," Charlie said.

"Right," Aaron said. "And speaking of that, you should use the manual trimmers to clean up all of the bushes and the hedges all around the property. It does a lot for your definition."

* * *

Once they'd finished with their yard work and they'd both taken a shower, Aaron and Charlie reported to Sonia as she'd directed. Sonia stood before them, observing the two boys who were standing at attention, each wearing a bath towel wrapped around their waist. Charlie was doing his best to follow Aaron's lead in being still and attentive. Sonia was wearing a short cream-colored silk robe, tied at the waist, which reminded Charlie that his ex-wife had an impressive figure.

"Aaron, Charlie, I want you both to come to my bedroom," she said. "Once there, you'll receive further instruction. And you won't need the towels."

"Yes, Mistress Sonia," Aaron replied.

"Yes . . . Mistress Sonia," Charlie replied.

Charlie noticed that Aaron immediately pulled off his bath towel and proceeded to Sonia's bedroom completely naked aside from his chastity cage. Charlie looked down for a moment. He wondered if he was prepared to serve his ex-wife in the manner she would demand. Then he took a deep breath, removed his towel, and followed Aaron. He couldn't imagine what Sonia was going to do.

"Aaron," Sonia began, once she had both boys standing at attention in her bedroom, "I have been considering the ways in which I may have failed in being consistent with Charlie, resulting in nothing but misery for him. I don't want to commit the same mistakes in my handling of you. Therefore, I'm going to institute the regular punishment of your beautifully formed and sculpted body. You will accept this as a gift of loving discipline, and as an opportunity for you to show surrender to my command."

"Yes, Mistress Sonia," Aaron said.

"As for Charlie," she said, "your public humiliation and punishment were both deeply satisfying for me to observe, but it wasn't enough. I'm nowhere near done with you. It has been a source of aggravation for me to have endured your little tantrum that so rightfully ended with you being made to submit to the authorities. It has been an annoyance to me that you did not see that *I am the authority.* You should have been mature enough to recognize that you should have listened to me. I have no interest in being nice about this. You've been remanded to my custody because I wanted it so. I have the power to make such things happen. You are now entirely dependent on me for my signature each week, signing off on your paperwork. I am not going to make this easy for you. Rather, it will be the opposite. So here are the rules: You will be naked, aside from your cage. I know you never liked wearing a chastity cage, so you're going to be locked up continuously in the tightest device possible. It gives me a great deal of satisfaction seeing your penis locked up tight. Just know that every interaction I have with you will be with your cage clearly visible to me. I will get so much enjoyment seeing you having to endure the humiliation I know you will feel. I deserve to witness your endless embarrassment while you strive to placate me. While you serve. So now, Charlie, I want to see you submit. I want you to get onto the bed, positioned on your hands and knees. I want to see you mindful of raising your butt up toward me to receive the paddle. Do so now," she said.

    Charlie still felt the sting of his caning when he climbed onto the bed and positioned himself on his hands and knees, taking care to offer his ass in the way she had indicated.

Sonia stood beside the bed, then crawled onto its surface and placed one hand on Charlie's back. The other held the long wooden paddle to his bare ass.

"Count off twenty for me, Charlie," she said.

He thought that at least it would not hurt as much as the cane. However, once Sonia had begun, he realized that she was not going to be lenient with him. He counted off the prescribed twenty strokes of the paddle, endeavoring to sound as grateful as possible.

"See, Charlie, that wasn't so bad," Sonia said. "And it makes a nice, rosy blush on your rear end. And now," Sonia said as she climbed off the bed, "I want you to kneel here, facing the bed." Sonia pointed to an area of the floor against the wall. She watched as Charlie complied with the order and assumed the position on his knees, and she could see the trepidation on his face. She smiled, wondering how she could have ever been lax in ordering Charlie to his knees, as she thought it seemed like such a natural position for him.

Then Sonia stood before Aaron, and to Charlie's surprise, she unlocked his chastity device. She guided him onto the bed, and began to rake Aaron's lean, muscular torso with her fingernails as she sunk her teeth into his pectoral muscle, biting him on the chest. Her hips began to thrust, grinding her pussy against his hip. She had one hand on his neck while the other left crimson stripes from her nails dragged across his naked body, intermittently grabbing and squeezing him as her mouth fed hungrily on his bare chest. Then she kissed him with the same carnivorous intensity.

Aaron knew only to surrender, his back arching in response to the pain and ecstasy of her sensual onslaught, her sexually dominant attack on his naked body. At times, Sonia's hand would find itself at the base of his erection, and it would suddenly, without warning, wrap tightly around its shaft.

"I'm sure that it's not lost on you, Charlie, that Aaron's cock is impressive in not only size, but also in its hardness," Sonia said.

She gripped him tightly, clamping down in a merciless submission hold.

"Hmmm, I so love the scent of hot, young, obedient cock," Sonia practically growled.

Aaron felt himself attempting to surrender to her domination of his body, but she anticipated his every movement, so that he was unable to submit any more than he already had.

"I want to reward you and your obedience by letting you fuck me, Aaron," Sonia said.

She laid back on the bed, untied her silk robe, and spread her long, elegantly shaped legs for him. He responded by positioning himself between her thighs and placing his cock against her soft, wet labia.

"I've never . . ." he began to say.

"I know," she said with a smile.

Aaron began fucking her, overwhelmed by the pleasure of driving his cock into her in a perpetual rhythm. She placed one hand on his neck, and the other on his left butt cheek, feeling the rhythmic pulse of his body as he gave himself to the ecstatic pleasure of her sex.

Charlie watched Aaron fucking Sonia, and he felt a sense of longing and desire. His chastity device was actively restraining his penis from becoming erect.

Aaron fell into a slow, sensual rhythm, while Sonia now held him by his hips and butt, feeling his deep, powerful thrust into her body. The scent and the sensation of her body made Aaron salivate, making his mouth wet in anticipation. Without warning, his body gave in to the extreme pleasure of fucking her and he began to ejaculate.

"Oh my god, I'm so sorry," he exclaimed. "I couldn't stop it."

"I know," she said with a warm smile.

When Aaron at last came to rest, she had him roll over to one side of her body on the bed.

"Charlie, come here," Sonia said, pointing to the floor at the foot of the bed.

Charlie was trembling, feeling a conflicting variety of emotions as he lowered himself into position.

"Aaron, to be fair, has never been allowed to fuck me before, so he lost control and unloaded his cum into my pussy," Sonia said. "Now you, Charlie, are going to lick it up."

He lowered his face between her thighs, and he began licking her, lapping Aaron's cum from her dripping wet slit while she reveled in the pleasure of his attentive tongue. Sonia held Aaron against her and started kissing him and caressing his naked body. She would occasionally stroke his cock, and it wasn't long before he was completely hard again.

"What do you think, Aaron?" Sonia asked. "I think Charlie's made my pussy all clean again for you. Would you like to try again to see if you can hold out longer this time?"

"Yes, Mistress Sonia," Aaron replied.

"Good boy," Sonia said affectionately.

Chapter 19

"Something I don't know about you, is how you first came to really know your place as a boy," Violet said. She was sitting on the sofa in her dorm room, with Theo kneeling on the floor before her.

"It was obvious from an early age that women are naturally gifted in assuming leadership roles," Theo said. "Their mental capabilities advanced so much more quickly than ours. It wasn't a mystery why they'd ascend to positions of power. And they would allow us to serve at their command only if we demonstrated the capacity for being compliant."

"Well, as you know, my doctoral thesis is also about the theory of segregated genders in education," Violet said. "I don't weigh in on what I believe so much as I just look at the evidence we have on the matter. Personally, I think it's good for boys to have females in the classroom to inspire them in a variety of ways. And their humiliation is part of it. They are obviously going to feel humiliated by their female counterparts in the comparison of their academic achievement."

"That was definitely the case," Theo replied. "I remember one day in a class called Social Dynamics; I was called on to weigh in by the teacher. It didn't happen often that a boy would be asked to contribute to the discussion, as we are better suited to listening while the female students speak among themselves. Anyway, I stated that I thought that women are better suited to positions of power. The teacher said that I was entirely incorrect, explaining that my use of the word *better* implies that those of the male gender are in any way suited to wielding power, and that the female is, by comparison, more so. She informed me that this is wrong, and that the male gender is not at all capable of handling the demands that holding power entails. I felt deeply embarrassed of my error, and the women in the class were instrumental in correcting me on this point. So it was to my benefit to feel humiliated in the moment to guide my thinking on the matter."

"Interesting," Violet said. "Yeah, that interaction is what I believe is valuable to the education of boys, the resultant humiliation by the female students."

"I remember that the young women at school would sort of experiment with their domination of the male students," Theo said. "They'd start with little things, assigning us tasks we were to perform for them. They were tests, I guess, to see if we could be effective in carrying out their orders. There was a game called Who's My Little Bitch, where any of the boys who thought they might be up to the challenge would compete, essentially, to see who could best accomplish the assignments given out by the females in the class."

Violet laughed.

"That's hilarious," she said.

"It was a fun game, really," he said. "They'd make it challenging, like getting something from the teacher's desk, where we'd get in trouble if we were caught. Something where there was the threat of punishment."

"Of course, you boys got punished, didn't you?" she asked.

"At the time, I wasn't a big fan of the reinstatement of punishment for boys," he said, "but I would eventually come to appreciate it. I'm grateful now for having been punished for my misbehavior."

"In situations where boys are given the option of choosing punishment by being given the strap, or the paddle, or the birch rod, or conversely, a suspension or detention, boys will consistently choose a physical punishment," Violet said. "They intuitively know that they truly deserve to feel the humiliation and pain of an immediate pants-down punishment, and that it is most effective in not only correcting their behavior, but it is a way for them to show contrition. They want to be well-behaved, and showing humility in accepting their fate is usually seen as preferable to them."

"The punishment we received was always pants down," Theo said. "Then we'd be given the strap."

"Oh, nice," she said. "That's effective."

"Definitely effective," he said. "Ms. Darling had an arm on her."

"Your teacher's name was Ms. Darling?" she asked, sounding amused.

"Yeah, and she was really strict with us," he said. "She really focused on the humiliation aspect of the punishment. She felt it was an important element in correcting our behavior."

"She was not wrong," Violet said. "I've spent time researching the use of corporal punishment in the academic arena. In places where it is mandated that boys receive consistent, pants-down punishment, they see an improvement in the behavior of the male students. It's no surprise, really, that when a boy understands that he'll receive a humiliating punishment across his bare butt in front of the class, they behave better. They focus better. And it turns out that it has a positive effect on the female students as well. It's sort of a stress relief for them just watching a boy take a beating. It can be cathartic for them, and it's a form of entertainment, of course, just a little break from the daily grind of schoolwork. And since a number of the young women in the class will one day be responsible for disciplining a boy of their own, it's actually educational."

"I do recall that the female students always seemed to treat it as a fun diversion, or like you said, an entertainment," Theo said.

"I really liked that when it happened, and we got to watch you boys get what you deserved," Violet said. "But women also know that it's good for you boys to be brought to heel. We'd come to learn that when boys have a clear set of expectations, they will make better choices about their behavior. When they have an understanding of what to expect if they behave in a certain way, they have an opportunity to act appropriately. The goal is to create a deterrent, to prevent a continuation of their misbehavior."

She examined Theo for a moment.

"OK, I know what I want to see right now," Violet said as she jumped up and crossed the room to get a large, pink-and-black box from her closet. "To answer any of your questions, I'll just say that my aunt is a crazy woman. And I guess she was actually right."

She set the box down on the coffee table, then pulled from the box a truly massive dildo, almost preposterous in size, yet sculpted realistically with a pair of balls and with a suction cup base. Theo's eyes widened. Violet laughed.

"So, my aunt gave me this," she said. "She explained that I should have a boy demonstrate his obedience by making him take it in the ass. I laughed it off at the time. She's always bought me really weird gifts. And I brought it to school with me because I didn't want to hurt her feelings, but I thought it was a really stupid present at the time."

She put the dildo down on the coffee table, attaching the suction cup to the surface.

"Until now," she said. Violet stood back and made a gesture toward the dildo she'd mounted to the table. "Now, I want to see you impress me. You'll mount the dildo and take its full length, until you can press your bare butt onto the surface of the table."

Theo swallowed hard.

"So, Theo, why don't you drop your pants?" Violet said, turning toward him.

"You mean—" he began.

"Is that hesitation, Theo?" Violet asked. "I'm not going to tell you twice."

"Yes, Violet," Theo said in response.

Theo began to take off his clothes.

"Oh my god it's huge," Theo said in a voice just above a whisper. "Will it even fit?"

"No, that's the challenge," Violet said, "you have to *make* it fit. Come on, it'll be fun. It's definitely going to be entertaining to watch," she said with a wide smile.

She opened a bottle of lubricant and began making the entirety of the dildo slick and wet.

"OK, first, I want you to show me that you're ready," Violet said. "I want you to get on your knees and elbows, then lower your forehead to the floor with your arms stretched out, hands flat on the floor."

Theo assumed the position she'd described.

"This is the best position for your body," Violet said. "It helps you focus your attention. Your hands are extended outward, away from you, in offering yourself to a higher purpose. Your head is down, forehead touching the floor in a show of humility. It demonstrates your willingness to submit your mind, and your very identity in service of a more elevated existence. Your knees are touching the floor, which is always a good look for a boy. But most importantly, you are offering up your ass for what corrective punishment is deemed necessary. That is the reason your back should have a bow shape to it, and your hips should be rotated somewhat. Your asshole is made vulnerable, as are your balls. Which is preferable, really. And your penis is exposed, but not obviously so. One may ignore its presence. What I want you to do is to assume this position often, not only to display your full, unconditional surrender to me, but to help form in your own mind the appropriate attitude you should adopt and conform to."

Violet placed her hand on Theo's butt, caressing his skin and feeling the firm, rounded musculature.

"I'm of the opinion that you can tell a lot about a boy when you have him offer his asshole," Violet said. "The way he positions his body is very telling. It shows if he is sincere in his submission. For instance, I'll look at the curve, or the arch in his back. It presents his asshole in a way that really looks like a surrender. I find that attractive."

She lubricated two fingers and slid them into his asshole.

"I do love penetration that is coercive in its size, massive in both length and girth," she said. "Boys should *want* an overwhelmingly enormous dildo violating their asshole to keep them in line. I won't hesitate in reaming your ass good and hard. It helps you to remain focused on your obligation to serve."

She removed her fingers and gave him a slap across his butt.

"Now, up on the table, cutie pie," she said.

Theo climbed up onto the coffee table, on his knees, and positioned himself above the dildo.

"Wait," Violet said. "Do you ever think about wanting me to unlock you? Do you think about me playing with your penis?"

"Sometimes," Kylan's admitted.

"Thank you for being honest with me," Violet said. "Does it feel frustrating for you? When you want it?"

"It makes me question my motivation, I guess," he replied. "Like, I wonder why my body expresses itself that way. I know that it's just paying tribute to you, and how much I desire you. It's symbolic of my devotion to you as your servant."

Violet smiled.

"I'm curious," she said. "I want you unlocked."

Theo had a sudden feeling of panic, like she was suggesting something dirty or wrong. Violet pulled the key from between her breasts and took its chain from around her neck. She slid it into his lock, then pulled the device off of his penis and testicles. Theo gasped at the sensation of being unlocked before Violet, as though he was undressed for the first time in her presence. It required his restraint to not reflexively cover himself. He felt his penis react.

"Oh," Violet said, but the word she'd spoken didn't so much end as it slowly vanished, leaving her mouth in the shape she'd originally made to pronounce it.

Theo's penis grew quickly into an erection that seemed to command ownership of his hips, as though his lower body was in support of his long, thick, and now fully erect cock.

"Theo," Violet said in a whisper.

She slowly raised her eyes to meet his.

"So, you didn't mention?" she asked.

"I'm sorry, mention?" he asked.

"That you have a big fat cock?" she asked. "I just never, I didn't realize I'd never unlocked it, which, I just thought it was . . . I don't know, I didn't think you were small, like tiny or anything. But I didn't know about *this*."

"I don't know if this is good or bad," Theo replied.

Violet laughed, which seemed to break the spell.

"It's, well, it's interesting, I guess," she said. "Wow. So, Theo, my servant boy, has a big fucking dick. Amazing. OK, this doesn't change the fact that I still, in fact, even more, I want to see you fucking what I thought was an enormous dildo, but now I see that it's not that much bigger than you are."

Violet sat down on the sofa.

"Take it in the ass, Theo," she commanded.

Theo lowered himself onto the tip of the dildo, aligning the well-lubricated cock head against his asshole. He relaxed his body as much as he could, then allowed the bulbous cock head to penetrate his ass. He gasped at the size of it, trying not to clench his muscles in response. He looked at Violet, who was watching with intense interest, staring at his erect cock as he slowly resumed lowering himself onto the shaft of the dildo.

"It always amazes me to see how much boys like being fucked in the ass," Violet said. "I guess it's a matter of maturity. Boys who understand their obligation to submit and embrace their servant status love anal penetration. But now I need to study your cock," Violet said.

Violet got up off of the sofa and straddled the coffee table, facing Theo. She placed her fingertip against the underside of his erect cock. As he rode up and down on the dildo, his cock rubbed against her finger.

"That feels nice, doesn't it?" she asked.

"It feels amazing," he replied.

"And what will happen if you come without my permission?" she asked.

"I will receive a hard punishment," he replied.

"Hmmm," she murmured. "Super hard. It's good that you know that. "Seriously, I was under the impression that you had a cute little penis. Small and submissive. You're going to have a new set of rules, Theo. I have to think about what punishment you've got coming to you as a result."

"Yes, Violet," he replied.

"So tell me. I assume you've long been embarrassed about having an enormous penis."

"Yes," he admitted.

"And I assume you were found out?" she asked. "Or were you able to hide it? I mean, you've managed to keep it hidden from me."

"There was this one young woman in my class," he explained, "her name was Kayla, and she was, well, at the time I thought she was mean. I've come to think of it differently now. She was just exercising her right to become an effective leader. She sat up front, so when the boys were punished, she had a front row seat. It was shortly after I'd been called to the front of the class for correction that she began teasing me about how I'd never fit in my chastity cage."

"Because of your size?" she asked. "I mean, even then?"

"Well, you know how you said that you developed early?" he asked.

"Oh, I see," she said. "But you hadn't gotten your first chastity device yet?"

"No, shortly after, but not at that time," he said. "So, Kayla would make fun of me," he said. "Taunting me about how I would need a specially designed cage for my big fat penis, as she called it, and even then, she said, it was going to be really tight on me. But the thing is, it was good for me, ultimately, because it really made me focus on being able to adjust to a really small device. I wanted to prove her wrong."

"Well, since you have a big fat dick, I am going to have to dominate you so much harder," Violet said. "You're in so much trouble, you've no idea. I am going to whip that tight little ass of yours until you can't sit down for a week. Do you hear me? Do you understand how much I'm going to make you suffer for me? I have absolutely no sympathy for how hard I'm going to make you pay for having a big fucking dick."

Theo was still riding the dildo for Violet when she had him hold his ass in position for her.

"Stick your butt out for me. Your beating starts now," she said.

Violet took a leather strap in hand and began whipping Theo hard across the ass. She'd meant what she'd said, and was merciless in giving Theo a hard punishment, laying the strap across his bare butt repeatedly, turning his skin bright red in the process.

"This is what you get, Theo," she said. "This is how it's going to be from now on."

After Violet whipped Theo's ass, she let him climb off of the enormous dildo.

"Now, I want you in my shower," she said.

"It's nice to have a private shower," Theo said once the water had reached the temperature Violet preferred.

They got in and let the warm water pour down over their naked bodies.

"Oh, right, you boys have an open shower room," Violet said. "Do women ever just walk in while you're showering?"

"Yes, sometimes," he replied. "Generally, it's for a reason, like they're looking for someone."

"Do they ever just, you know, watch?" she asked.

"My friend Aaron told me that your friend Serena does that," he said. "She will just walk in and stand there watching him."

"Yeah, she has a thing for him, but he can't with her because of Sonia. She has some other boy, but I guess she wants Aaron as well."

Violet kissed Theo on his chest.

"So, you remember the thing I said about the website? Slow Ride?" Violet asked. "I've changed my mind. The thing is, it's really just a fantasy for me," she said. "I love the thought of putting you on display, but then I think about other women seeing you and I realize that I just want you on display for me. Plus, you're too big. They want tiny little penises, way smaller than the dildo."

"Yeah, that's correct," he replied.

"Did you just say, 'that is correct' to me?" she asked. "Since when has anything I've said not been correct?"

"I apologize," he replied. "I misspoke."

"You're right on the edge of earning yourself a spanking across the head of your penis," she said. "It's size, now fully revealed to me, does not change my ownership."

She wrapped her arms around him and held him tightly.

"Because it's mine," she said, and pressed her head against his chest.

She stood still for a moment, feeling the water pouring down over their naked bodies. Theo's erection was pressed against her belly.

"I want nothing more than to be your property, Violet," he replied.

"Of course you do, cutie pie," Violet said. "And I have every reason to believe that you'll show absolute obedience to my command," she said. "I mean, really no different than always, but with greater purpose."

"Yes, Violet," he replied.

Chapter 20

"I have an idea," Violet said. "You know what would look so cute on you? I'm thinking back to the night when I first saw you. And I am trying *not* to think about the way my brother Cary looked when I took you to visit my family," she said, laughing.

"What, he looked really good, I think," Theo said.

"Yeah, it's just that he's my brother," she said. "Did you know that the woman he's seeing now, Isabella, she got Cary a job as a model for these ultra-tight chastity devices? He told me that they just have him pose for photos wearing each of the devices because they think he has the right build for it. The photos are pretty close to just being naked, which will probably be good for getting him out of his comfort zone, you know? He needs something like that. He needed a woman like Isabella."

Violet began looking through her dresser drawers in search of the right item of clothing.

"I think it would be fun to have you in a tight little pair of panties without your chastity cage," she said. "Come on, how fun is that? So daring, so scandalous," she said with a laugh.

Suddenly, she located what she had been looking for.

"A-ha!" she exclaimed.

She held up a pair of tiny pink thong panties, with small bows on either hip.

"These will *not* fit you oh-so-perfectly," she said triumphantly. "Put them on."

Theo pulled the panties on and modeled them for her.

"You look spectacular," she said, smiling broadly, a brilliant smile that made clear her approval. "Turn around."

Theo turned.

"Perfect," Violet said. "I so love spanking your tight little butt, and the fact that you're wearing thong panties means, well, you know. You so badly want to get a spanking. No one will think you're not my little bitch now," she added, teasing him. "But one more thing."

She placed a collar around his neck.

"There," she said, standing back to survey his body. "But you know what would really make clear your status in relation to me, is a leash. I think boys look nice like that. It shows that a boy respects his position in relation to his owner. And I'm your owner, aren't I?

"I hope so," he replied.

"So, what should it be?" she said, thinking out loud, "a leash attached to the collar around your neck? Or a leash attached to a tight little ball strap? That'd look good on you, wouldn't it? You'd look so completely dominated, a good look for a boy, if I were to lead you around by the balls. I'd keep the leash nice and short. A quick little flick of my wrist would keep you on your toes," she said, laughing at the thought. "Just think about how good you'd look with a leash attached to your ball strap. It would be impressive, don't you think?"

"Yes, Violet," he replied.

"Good," she said. "I love it when you submit."

She retrieved a leather ball strap, then pulled his panties down in front and attached the strap around his balls. Then she attached a leash.

"You look cute with your big fat dick all hard and sticking out of your panties," Violet said. "I've always thought it impressive when a woman would have a slave unlocked and he would be getting erections all the time," she said, giggling at the thought. "It shows that she denies him a lot, and I'm always impressed with women who control their boys like that. It's nice to see a boy serving his owner with an irrepressible hard-on. It shows respect, I think. Plus, your panties look cute pulled down in front. I mean, it's probably embarrassing for you, but I like it even more because of that."

Violet reached out and touched the tip of his cock with her fingertip.

"This makes me think about that first time, when I found you downstairs at that house party," she said.

"Can I tell you something about that night?" Theo asked.

"Yes, and a punishment for you for not telling me before now," Violet said.

"It's just that I'd never had a woman cum on my face," he said. "I didn't know how you'd react to me mentioning it."

"Wait, you mean when I squirt when you make me orgasm?" she asked.

"Yes," he replied.

"Really?" she asked. "You'd never had a woman do that?"

"No, really, you were the first," he replied.

"Well, then I was just marking my territory," she said. "But I'm surprised that was your first. It was right in your mouth, which I remember because I was impressed, and it made me orgasm harder watching it. And you lapped it up like you knew what you were doing."

"I just knew to surrender," Theo said.

"Perfect," Violet said. "For me, it was like I'd found not only a boy to have in that position, but a place for you as well. I realized that your place was with me as my servant boy. And then it was like an exploration began, and I learned that I had underestimated my own ability to experience not only the physical pleasure of pussy worship, but the psychological, or holistic pleasure as well. That's when we had the *Sorry, not sorry* conversation when I told you that I was, I mean, we, were going to be spending a lot of time focused on what I was beginning to see as a deep, pun intended, exploration into my orgasmic potential. You were so cute and sweet to be so enthusiastic. And since then, I've learned so much about my body's response to your lips and tongue. I credit you for bringing so much talent to the table. Hence the *Not sorry* part. But the important part is that we continue, with you learning more and more as we go. I know that it is the best possible situation for you and your development as a servant to me. Like I was saying, part of it is the psychological benefit. When you spend time in worshipping my pussy, it allows me to think of your value to me in new and unique ways."

"I love that, Violet. I so love to worship your pussy," Theo said.

"Probably not as much as I love it," Violet said. "I mean, I love it when you're doing it."

"I am certain that I love it more than you do," he replied.

"That's not possible," she said.

"Why not?" Theo asked. "When I worship your pussy, I want nothing else in the world. I want it to last forever."

"I do appreciate your saying that," Violet said. "When I sit on your face, it really brings into sharp focus that you have absolutely no authority or control over anything. The vulva and the clitoris are best served by the tongue, and what a waste it would be to not have your tongue there to receive every delicious drop. And when I squirt, to not have your mouth open and ready when I cum on your face. It's really perfect, and I just dominate you so completely that it feels like I'm being generous in even considering your existence beyond your utility as a slave."

Theo felt a cool, electric, tingling feeling course through his body at the sound of the word *slave*.

Violet slid two lubricated fingers into his asshole, pushing them deep inside of him.

"I've begun to see your potential as not just a servant to me, but something even greater. Far, far lower in status, but more elevated in importance to me. I want to see how far it goes. I've decided that I do want to have you serve me like a slave," she said.

"A slave?" he asked.

"Yes, Theo," she said. "My slave. You will serve me as you have been doing, you will kneel before me, and you will obey. But now you will do so as my slave, thinking only of me and my desires. You will want only what I want."

"That is," Theo said, smiling, "what I want."

"Very funny," Violet said, "but no, you no longer want anything. You simply obey my command. You don't just recognize female power. You worship female power. And when we are around my friends, I want them to know that you'll take correction without hesitation and definitely without complaint. So when we are around them, do not hesitate if I order you to assume the position for punishment. Do you understand?"

"Yes, Violet," he replied.

Violet observed him for a moment, then placed her hand on the back of his neck and pulled him toward her to kiss him, sliding her tongue into his mouth while she kept her fingers deep inside his ass.

"My slave," she said softly. "Now, if I take you as my slave, you'll have only to follow orders, as expected, but I will want more," she said. "I will expect your complete subjugation to my authority. You will need to do as I say immediately, without question and without hesitation. And I will expect you to exceed this relatively simple requirement by going above and beyond in your service and attention. Anticipate my needs."

"Yes, Violet, thank you," Theo replied.

Violet brought Theo toward her body, and he began kissing her neck, slowly moving down her body. He lingered momentarily in licking and sucking her nipples, which would become prominently erect, both her areola and her nipple. The scent of Violet's body had become, for Theo, something that made him feel not only aroused, sexually, but it also gave him a feeling of contentment. It felt like home in that he knew his place was there with her. He never felt so certain of his belonging to any particular place and time than when her legs were spread to admit him, and her thighs were to either side of his broad shoulders.

Violet was not still. She did not passively accept pleasure. She was active in her expression of ecstasy, moving her hips, thrusting them toward Theo's face, moving her legs, occasionally clamping them together tightly on either side of his head, moving her feet along either side of his torso, placing them on his lower back. Her hands were employed in grabbing handfuls of his hair, pressing his face against her body, or taking her large, round breasts in her hands and pinching her nipples.

She rolled over and offered Theo her butt to worship. He took hold of a pillow, and she raised her hips as he pulled it into place beneath her, raising her hips and ass toward him. His hands took hold of her hips as though taking possession of her body while he kissed her butt cheeks in a way that felt like an expression of his adoration of her. He began licking and kissing the top of the crevice between her butt cheeks, then moved downward, slowly. She reached back to bring his lips between her between her butt cheeks. His tongue began lavishing her asshole with long, sensual licks. Theo slid the tip of his tongue inside of her asshole and pressed his lips against her body. He kissed and licked her, his tongue gradually extending farther, penetrating her deeper.

"That's perfect," Violet said. "I so love it when you show me how much you love worshiping my ass."

For what length of time neither of them would have been able to guess, Theo's tongue became serpentine in its slow, sensuous rhythm, worshipping Violet's ass in a breathtaking display of his adoration and desire. Theo thought that it was perhaps the most valuable and beautiful gift that Violet offered to him was that he was allowed to worship and serve her. He'd always thought of himself as a tool to be used in service of the female gender, and he felt it such a privilege to be used as such in providing pleasure to Violet. He heard her make a small sighing sound, to which he responded by placing his hand on her pussy, and he began using two fingers to stroke her clit, eventually bringing her to orgasm while his tongue was deep inside her ass.

* * *

"Theo, I've decided on an arrangement where you will surrender what few rights you have as a male to me and become my slave," Violet said.

She had Theo kneeling before her without his chastity cage, but he still wore the leather ball strap with a leash attached. Otherwise, he was naked, hard, and obedient.

"By the way, I like the way that a boy looks when he's on his knees and he's fully erect, like so hard that it seems that it's his body is in service to his erection, you know?" she said. "But his knees spread wide, planted firmly, make it clear not just his body, but his mind as well is in service to me. Just waiting for me to give him a command."

Violet continued to examine his body, his attitude of obedience, and his apparent adoration of her. She drew the leash tight.

"So, about this arrangement," she continued. "You will be required to not just submit, but you will become my committed slave. I want to see what level of submission you are capable of offering me on a full-time basis. I will want to test your ability in providing personal service to me as not just your superior, but as a final authority over you. Do you understand?"

"Yes, Violet," he replied.

"Good," she said. "Because I will allow for no recourse in any objection you may have, though I can't imagine your being so arrogant as to have one. But like I said, you will have forfeited all rights to me. You will provide me with a spectacular, impeccable level of service and exhibit a breathtaking lack of ego in your submission to my authority."

She eyed him carefully.

"You know, I've had a few boys attempt to serve me before, and each of them ultimately failed to impress me," she admitted. "In each case, I finally just devised a very public humiliation for their punishment, then broke it off. I will add that all of them begged me to reconsider. They each left begging to continue being my slave. But I do not lower my standards for any reason. It is the boy's responsibility to measure up. Do you understand?"

"Yes, Violet," he replied.

"I've an assignment," Violet said. "What did you say the game was called? Who's the bitch?"

Theo smiled.

"It was called Who's My Little Bitch," he replied.

"Close enough," she said. "Now we find out. I want you to start stroking your cock for me. You can't come without permission, of course. But that doesn't mean that you can go slow. I want it to look sexy and hot, kind of desperate. I want to see long strokes from the base to the rim of your cock head. Now, who owns your cock?"

"You own my cock, Violet," Theo replied.

"Who decides if you come?" she asked.

"You decide if I come, Violet," he replied.

"Anyone else?" she asked.

"No, no one else can make that decision," he replied.

"And why is that, Theo?" she asked.

"Because you own my cock," he replied.

"I own all of you, Theo," she said. "Who's my little bitch?"

"I'm your little bitch," he replied.

"And why is that?" she asked.

"Because I am your slave," he replied.

"And why are you my slave, Theo?" she asked.

"Because you are the kindest, most generous and loving dominant female in all the world and you have gifted me with the privilege of serving you as your slave," he replied.

Violet smiled, then maneuvered closer to his body and took his cock in her hand. He placed his hands to his sides. She gripped his shaft tightly, squeezing it firmly in her fist. She could feel the heat emanating from his cock as it began to throb in her hand. She held his cock tightly in one hand, his leash in the other.

"Now, Theo," she said. "Now, you may come."